# SKY
# RUN

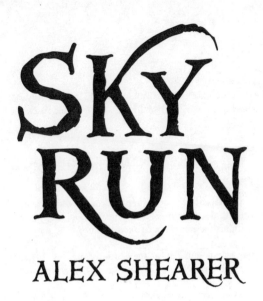

# SKY RUN

## ALEX SHEARER

HOT
KEY
BOOKS

First published in Great Britain in 2013 by Hot Key Books
Northburgh House, 10 Northburgh Street, London EC1V 0AT

A CIP catalogue record for this book is available from the British Library.

Hardback ISBN: 978-1-4714-0048-3
Paperback ISBN: 978-1-4714-0084-1
EBook ISBN: 978-1-4714-0050-6

1

Typeset by Palimpsest Book Production Limited, Falkirk, Stirlingshire
This book is set in 11pt Sabon LT Std

Printed and bound by Clays Ltd, St Ives Plc

**FSC**

Hot Key Books supports the Forest Stewardship Council (FSC), the leading
international forest certification organisation, and is committed to printing
only on Greenpeace-approved FSC-certified paper.

www.hotkeybooks.com

Hot Key Books is part of the Bonnier Publishing Group
www.bonnierpublishing.com

# 1

# youngish for her age

**PEGGY'S STORY:**

I was one hundred and twenty years old last birthday. Which is a good age in some places, though it's not so much round here. But it's no time of life to be looking after teenagers. I can tell you that.

I've got two of them. Not that they're mine, not exactly. Indirectly though, I guess. They're somehow related – great-grands, or great-great-grands, or several times removed, or I don't know what. But anyhow, I got saddled with them.

That's the thing about relatives, they can always track you down. At least they can when they want something. They're not so hot on *you* tracking *them* down when *you* want something. They're better at avoiding you then.

I've been farming this middle-of-nowhere rock for at least sixty years. My closest neighbour is over the way, on the next island. He's near enough to shout at, and far enough away to ignore if I feel like it. Which I do. Frequently. And the feeling's mutual.

But essentially, if there was a place called Nowhere, then this would be the middle of it. It's not called the Outlying Settlements for nothing.

We're so far off the Main Drift that we don't get visitors from one turning to the next, except perhaps for the occasional Cloud Hunter. Sometimes I buy water from them, sometimes I don't – I've got my own condenser here, but it's old and not so reliable.

Those Cloud Hunters, and one or two of my neighbours from across the way, are the only people I see round here. And the locals are the same as me, mostly – old and crotchety. Though it's fine here as long as you've got your health and teeth. But as soon as that goes, well, you're gone with it.

My immediate neighbour, old Ben Harley over there, he's not so much crotchety as cantankerous. But I know he's looking out for me, same as I'm looking out for him – if only to have the pleasure of burying him first.

Other than that, I don't get many callers. I was married once but he died and I decided not to try it twice. I had three children, but they went off into the world, and I moved here. I staked a claim on this piece of rock and no one contested it – probably because no one else wanted it – and I've been here ever since.

I've outlived everyone now – my daughters and my son. It's a strange thing to outlive your children. It feels all topsy-turvy and the wrong, unnatural way round. You even feel you've done them an injustice somehow, and you should have had the decency to predecease them.

But then – as people are so fond of saying – whoever said life was fair? They say that so much I wonder if somebody *did* actually once say that life was fair, and it's down to everyone else to disprove and contradict the statement.

So anyway, that's how I go on, turning after turning. I grow fruit and vegetables in the greenhouse; I put the nets out to catch a few sky-fish. For company, I've got the sky-puss here – though he's the next best thing to useless and all he does is eat – and I've got a sky-seal parked on the far side of the island. I didn't invite him and he stinks. But I can't seem to get rid of him, and even when I do, he just comes back again.

The island isn't huge, but it's home. It would take you a day to walk around it, if you weren't rushing, so there's room to stretch your legs. I've got solar panels for power and I can communicate over a reasonable distance with the cell phone, but that's about it.

So here I am, when one day I spot a sky-boat heading in this direction. I didn't think all that much about it, as people often pass by on their way to somewhere. It's the stopper-offers we don't get.

As the boat approaches, old sky-puss here actually bestirs himself and gets up onto his own six feet. (Don't ask; it's how they're made.) They're curious creatures, sky-cats, but bone idle. It takes something unusual or something exceptionally tasty to get them off their backsides.

My own boat's tied up at the jetty there. It's of the style known as a sky-runner – though sky-plodder might be more accurate, as it's a workhorse, not a racer. It won't take you anywhere fast, but it will get you there in the end – if it gets you there at all, and if it doesn't, well, you probably won't have missed much.

So, I wondered what was coming in that morning. It didn't look like the mail boat – though it had been a while since I'd had a letter. But then I got a sight of the compressors and the scarred faces and the tattoos and I knew that it was a bunch of Cloud Hunters. But not just them, for they appeared to have two faces among them that didn't bear those scars, nor the dark, suntanned skin, nor the various bangled adornments and badly advised piercings.

These two sore thumbs were pasty-faced and unhealthy-looking, like they'd spent too long in darkened rooms and not playing outside like you're supposed to for the avoidance of rickets. And they were young, by the look of them, five or six, maybe seven at the most, a boy and a girl.

As the cloud-hunting boat drew near, I went and stood on a rock and called to them.

'Got all the water I need right now, friend,' I said. (It pays to be friendly out here, because you never know when you're going to need one.) 'Tanks are full and I won't be requiring any for a while. Call again in another half-turning. I wouldn't bother landing. Don't want to waste your time.'

Usually that would have been enough, and those Cloud Hunters would have kept going. But not today.

'We're going to have to dock, Peggy,' the man at the

4

helm called over, and I knew him then, as I'd bought water from him a few times. His name was Kaleir, or something – they all have weird names like you never heard before; I think they spend the long, empty evenings making them up – and he had all the usual arm bracelets and face scars and tattoos, and three unnecessary earrings, where one would have done. But then, Cloud Hunters were never ones for understatement.

'You got problems?' I asked, as I watched the sky-boat sail in and prepared to throw him a rope.

'Not more than the usual,' he said. 'I've got something for you though.'

'And what's that?'

But he didn't answer.

They drifted in and he closed the sails and we tied the boat up at the jetty. As well as Kaleir there was a woman on board, plus their own two children, as well as the other two – who were pale as sheets in comparison. Last time I'd seen anything so wan-looking, it had been living under a boulder.

'So where you headed?' I asked, more for the sake of something to say than out of real interest.

'Wherever the clouds are, Peggy,' Kaleir said.

'Well, they're not round here.'

'No, not yet, but the tracker says they're coming.'

And he gesticulated with his thumb to a third individual, who was sitting on the deck, eating a plate of sky-shrimp with fast-moving chopsticks, and who had the distinction of being the only fat Cloud Hunter I had ever seen. Usually

5

they tend towards slim and athletic, but he was the exception to the rule. He had the bracelets; he had the scars; he had the tattoos. But he also had about forty kilos too much blubber. But maybe eating was his hobby.

'So what can I do for you?' I said, as they started coming down the walkway.

'Tanuk, bring the children,' Kaleir said, and the fat one stuck his chopsticks behind his ear – along with the toothpick already there – and shooed the two pasty-looking kids along, helping them gather up their belongings, of which there weren't many.

'Hold on,' I said. 'Just hold it there. I don't know who gave you the idea that I was in the market for kids, but they told you wrong. I'm one hundred and twelve years old, and bringing kids up is one thing I'm done with for good. So thanks, but no thanks.'

'No option, Peggy,' Kaleir said. 'I've been charged with delivering them to you, and here they are.'

'Then you can put them right back on that cloud-hunting boat of yours and take them away again.'

By this time the two kids were walking up the jetty with the fat tracker waddling behind them. They looked a bit lost and apprehensive and I couldn't blame them. If I'd been six years old and I'd suddenly met me, I'd be feeling apprehensive as well.

'That's far enough,' I said. And I stood there, blocking the way.

'Well,' Kaleir said, 'these two are for you, Peggy –'

'Just told you,' I said. 'I don't want them.'

6

He didn't listen. Cloud Hunters don't. Not when they're averse to what they're hearing.

'And this is for you also,' he said. 'This comes with them.'

He handed me a bag, a kind of leather satchel. I opened it up and inside was some money in notes – a lot of money – and a letter.

'What's this?'

'You'd better read it.'

'Have you read it?'

'I can't read,' Kaleir said, and without the slightest trace of embarrassment too, just matter-of-fact, the way somebody might have said 'I can't swim', or 'I can't play the piano', like it was no big commotion at all.

I took the letter and opened it up.

'Dear Mrs Mackinley –'

Well, I resented that for a start. Mackinley died sixty years ago, and here people are, still calling me by his name. I told them round at City Hall that I was reverting to my own name, Piercey, but they never got the message or didn't listen. Of course, the island with City Hall on it is several weeks' sailing from here. It's the capital. Biggest island, largest population.

Anyway, I won't give you the whole blah-de-blah of the contents of the letter. It went on for several pages, and there were even further pages of supporting documentation, along with a family tree, lineage, various social security documents, copies of marriage, birth and death certificates, and the news that these two children in front of me had been orphaned by an unfortunate act of piracy on the high skies by persons unknown.

7

They had been found drifting on a life raft in the vicinity of the Isles of Night (which is a short cut you don't want to be taking, not unless you've got a large harpoon gun or a couple of Cloud Hunters with you for protection). Their parents were missing, presumed dead. Extensive enquiries had been made throughout the islands and no other next of kin had been found.

So I'm standing there reading this, still blocking the jetty – which is starting to look a little crowded by now – and looking up at me are these two faces, which seem like they're made out of unbaked dough, with raisin eyes full of both fear and suspicion and, strangely, a kind of innocent trust too.

Kaleir makes a move to walk around me and go on land.

'Hold it right there,' I say. 'I'm still reading.'

'Reading seems to take a long time,' he says.

'And thinking.'

'What's there to think about?' Kaleir says. 'You're kin, aren't you? So you take them and you look after them.'

'I'll judge that,' I tell him.

To be honest, what I'm thinking to myself is that, first, I don't know if I believe this story – supporting documentation or not; and second, even if it's true, I'm so removed in lineage from these two kids, they might as well be strangers.

Not only do I not know them, I don't even recognise the names of their parents. One of the names of the parents' parents I half know. But that's a pretty tenuous connection. But then, you see, that's City Hall on City Island for you. If they can avoid spending a cent on welfare, they'll do it. They fob off the needy on even the furthest away relative and they'll say, just like Kaleir had, that you're a blood relation, so it's your problem.

'Well?' Kaleir says. 'You letting us come on land so we can stretch our legs?'

'And get something to eat, maybe –' the tracker adds.

'Hold on,' I say. 'Why don't *you* have them?'

Kaleir looks at me and then at his wife and then back. 'Us?'

'Bring them up as Cloud Hunters,' I say. 'Why not? They'd look cute once you did the coming-of-age scars.' At which one of the kids winced and the other looked disgusted.

But Kaleir shakes his head.

'We can't,' he says. 'No blood link. Can't be.'

'I don't mind,' I say. 'I'll even sign the paperwork agreeing to let you have them. And you can keep the money.'

He looks at his wife, then at the tracker. I know he's tempted. Children are wealth to Cloud Hunters. I don't know why, because kids are a big expense, who keep you awake nights, and they're forever asking you how long it is until you get somewhere. But she shakes her head, as if to say it would be wrong.

'It wouldn't be right,' he says, taking his cue from her. 'They're yours. They should be brought up your way.'

'I don't have a way,' I say.

'You're a land-dweller, Peggy. We're nomads.'

'Makes no difference to me. So I'm telling you that either you take them and keep them, or you cart them back to where you found them.'

9

'Can't do that, Peggy.'

'Oh yes you can. City Hall paid you to find me, didn't they? So you just take them back and say I wasn't at home, or I died, or my little island here got blown out of orbit and disappeared. You needn't even make a special journey. Just drop them off next time you're in the vicinity. No problem.'

And it wouldn't have been. No problem at all. If the smaller of those two children – with their straw-coloured hair and their poor pasty faces – hadn't looked up at me and said,

'Granma, don't you want us?'

And started to cry. And you know what he does then, just to add insult to personal injury? He reaches out with both his small arms, and he gets me round the legs, so I can't even move or go a step away. While his sister stands next to him looking up at me too; but she's dry-eyed and more kind of practical, less emotional, and a little older than he is.

'Don't cry, Martin,' she says. 'It's OK. We've got each other.'

And so there I am – with it all so sweet and just as I like it on my little island, no responsibilities, no serious worries, just pleasing myself. But what do I do about this? There's the small one got me round the legs, crying his heart out. And there's his sister, about a year or eighteen months older I'm guessing, who's all ready to go away again and to do her damnedest to make sure the two of them survive. So there you have it – the brave and the pitiful; the pleading and the defiant.

And, on top of all this, I've got the Cloud Hunters

standing there looking at me, knowing that they're all so tightly knit in the family department that they'd never turn anyone away, not if it was the most distant cousin in the distant cousin universe.

So what am I do to?

Well, to be straight, that's what's called a rhetorical question, as I'm not asking it for an answer, I'm just asking it for effect.

You know what I do. It's that or you're stupid. So I did it. And that was eight years ago. And it even worked out a whole lot better than I thought. But, as I say, that was eight years ago, and now I'm eight years older. I was only one hundred and twelve years back then, which was no age, but now I'm getting to be old bones. And they were younger too, cute kids, biddable, persuadable, amenable, even grateful. I was the old and wise one then. But now, everything I know, they know it.

Fact is, I've got two teenagers on my hands. Well, one teenager and one near teenager. And, somehow, I've got to get them to school.

My problem is how. You see, I chose this island on the assumption that once I got settled here I would never have to leave. But now I do.

I've got the school places all arranged. It's boarding too. They can stay there until their education's finished, if need be. And all free. The government will pay. It's desperate for educated people now – thanks to past mistakes it made with that tight welfare budget. Only I have to get them there. That's all.

That's me, a one-hundred-and-twenty-year-old, and my boat there, which is rickety and only just on the right side of sky-worthiness, and two kids, one of whom's a full-time daydreamer, while the other thinks she knows everything, and she doesn't have a clue yet about how little that is.

And separating us from the happy-ever-after promised land are a couple of thousand kilometres of wilderness, and some of the most pirate-infested, nutcase-infested, dangerous-creature-infested, weirdo-infested and crazy-infested ships, boats, sky and islands that you'll ever see this side of the Main Drift. There are people out there who've been fighting each other so long they can't recollect why they're doing it, but they go on doing it anyway, if only from force of habit and lack of alternative occupation.

And there's us, and the old boat, and the harpoon gun, and three harpoons. And enough water and provisions to last us a few weeks. And there's some out-of-date sky-charts. And a fat, useless sky-cat with bad breath and a skin complaint.

And that's it.

So you'll understand – if you think about it – why I'm having a bad day and why the headaches and the leg rash have come back. But then – as the soldier tied to the post said, just before they shot him – the sun is shining and the sky is blue; what can possibly go wrong in such perfect conditions?

# 2

# private stash

**PEGGY'S STORY (CONTINUED):**

Fact is that the worst kind of ignorance is where you don't know what you don't know. And that's the problem with these two here. They don't know how ignorant they are.

Gemma's bolshie; Martin's less so, but he's moody or he's days away, and he can sit there not saying anything for hours on end, just dreaming of who knows what. What worries me is that he might not be thinking anything – just staring.

'What do we have to go for, Peg?' he wanted to know.

'To learn things,' I told him, for the umpteenth.

'I know enough.'

'No. You just think you do.'

'Yes, I do. I can sky-swim, sail a boat, skin a sky-shark, use a harpoon, condense water, grow stuff, eat stuff, cook, make clothes, survive, navigate, sail, repair things –'

'There's more to life than that.'

'Such as?'

'Plenty. You'll find out when you get to City Island.'

'But I don't want to go and find out. I want to stay here.'

'Well, you can't. You can't go giving up on the world until you've had something to do with it. You need to get educated.'

'I thought *you* were doing that,' Gemma butted in. 'You said.'

'I've taught you all I know,' I said. 'Which, admittedly, wasn't much to start with.'

'You've done all right, Gran.' (That's Martin, coming to my defence. Sometimes it's Peg he calls me, sometimes it's Gran. Sometimes it's more like: Who are you, do I know you?)

'Maybe, but life here is kind of narrow, Martin. You've got to go to school, see life, see the city –'

'What's a city?'

'I already told you. And that's one thing you'd better try getting the hang of.'

'What?'

'Paying attention.'

'And what do they do in schools anyway?'

'You sit in a room and they teach you things.'

'Sit in a room? I don't like sitting in rooms.'

'You'll get used to it.'

'I won't.'

'Just go and carry that sack of provisions down to the boat, will you?'

'OK.'

'You also need to meet other people your own age. You can socialise.'

'What's that?'

'It's getting to know people. You can have friends.'

'What's that?'

I just shooed him away to go and load up the boat. Then I said to his sister, 'And you'll meet boys.'

'What would I want to do that for?' she said. 'I've already met *him* –' she nodded towards the disappearing shape of her brother – 'and I'm not that impressed.'

'He's your brother,' I said. 'Other boys are different.'

'Well, I hope so.'

'You'll have different feelings about other boys.'

'Yeah – no doubt,' Gemma said. But she was a bit sneery about it. And they both used to be such charming little things too.

'Go and take the dry goods down to the boat, Gemma, please,' I said, and I handed her a sack of stuff.

We were all but ready to go. I was sitting studying sky-charts, as my navigation – while sound in principle – was rusty in practice. The last thing I wanted was us setting off for City Island and ending up in the Isles of Dissent, getting strung up by our thumbs by bigots for having the wrong kind of socks on – not that any of us had any socks, but you get my meaning.

There wasn't much to leave behind, to be sure. But just in case anyone happened by and took a fancy to the place, I was also in the process of putting up a big sign saying: This Island Occupied. Prop: Peggy Piercey. Land Registry Ownership No: PP184354005T.

It was all bull, of course. I'd just taken the place over

15

and hadn't registered it at all. But even if I had, it wouldn't make any difference to determined squatters. Not that you get so many of them in these parts. We're too far off the Main Drift and from what passes for civilisation.

Before we set sail on the big journey, I went on a short one to visit old Ben Harley over on the next island. He's younger than I am, but that's not the point. You can be old Ben at any age. You could even be born being old Ben. And boring old Ben at that.

'Hi, Ben,' I said, as the boat drifted in towards his jetty, and he stood there in neighbourly belligerence, welcoming me in with his harpoon gun.

'It's you, is it?' he said. 'What do you want, Peggy? If it's money, I don't have any. If it's tools, I don't lend them. If it's spare parts, I've used them all. If it's water, I don't have all that much. If it's anything else, I don't have any of that either.'

'I've just come to say goodbye, Ben.'

'Where you going?'

'And to ask a favour.'

'I don't have any.'

'I just want you to keep an eye on the place for me.'

'Well, I can do that, I guess.'

'I've put a sign up. But if anyone comes along looking to colonise my island –'

'I'll give them a taste of this,' he said, patting his trusty harpoon gun.

'Thanks.'

'So where are you going?'

'Like I told you, a while back.'

'When was that?'

'Last week.'

'I don't remember conversations from that far back. Yesterday, maybe . . . this morning, perhaps –'

'We were having some of your home-made at the time, remember?'

'I don't have none,' old Ben said, suddenly wary again and worried I might ask for a bottle of his home-brewed sky-weed whisky for the journey. It's strong stuff and actually tastes better than it sounds. Not, in all honesty, a whole lot better. And if you dab it on your skin, it's good for keeping the midges off.

'Well, remember it or not, I told you the two of them were growing up and I'd shown them all I knew and sooner or later I'd have to send them to school.'

'Ah. Right. So that's what you're doing?'

'That's it. I'm taking them there now. We're setting off today.'

Old Ben looked at me. He put down his harpoon gun and took out his pipe. He never smokes it. He just sticks it in his mouth, draws on it, and takes it out again for effect. He's had no tobacco for thirty years.

'Where you going? What school?'

'City Island. The boarding.'

'Can't they get the school bus?'

'Bus? Ben, there is no bus that comes all the way out here.'

'You sure about that? I thought otherwise.'

'It's make your own way or miss out.'

'So it's just you and them sailing?'

'Me and them.'

'One doddery old biddy and a couple of kids? And nobody with muscles?'

'Less of the doddery and less of the biddy. I'll let you have the kids. The muscles don't matter so much when you've got the brains. But you wouldn't know about that.'

'Peggy, don't take this the wrong way, but what do you reckon your chances are of getting there?'

'Pretty good.'

'I'd put them at about one in a thousand.'

'Thanks.'

'Unless you're going round the Main Drift?'

'No. I'm staying off it. I'm not going on the Main Drift in my little boat. What if some great water train of the United Fleet comes along, or a sky-whaler, and they don't see us?'

'So you're going through the bad lands?'

'We are taking the back roads, so to speak, yeah. But the bad lands, they aren't so bad.'

'Well, it was nice knowing you, Peggy. Not *that* nice, but –'

'Thanks.'

'How long shall I give it before I work out that you're not coming back?'

'Give it a turning. You can have my island if I'm not back by then.'

'No, thanks. One island's enough for me. I'm not empire-building. Anyway, you probably will be back. You're too old and ugly to live anywhere else.'

'That's right,' I said. 'And I clapped eyes on you and thought "here's someone who makes me look pretty by comparison". It's not everyone who's lucky enough to have a gargoyle for a neighbour.'

Old Ben even got all sentimental then – for him.

'Well, I shall miss you, Peg,' he said. 'No one to wave to of a morning.'

'I'll be back. Don't get too lonely.'

'Here,' he said. 'Let me give you a few supplies and some extra water.'

'I thought you didn't have any to spare.'

'It turned up of a sudden. And I'll give you a few bottles of sky-brew from the private stash.'

'Ben, all your stash is private. There's only you here.'

'You can never be too careful as to where you keep your liquor.'

So, not being proud, I took what he gave me. Then I shook old Ben by his hand – as kissing him on the whiskers was not a thing I could contemplate – and he promised to keep an eye on my island. So home I went, to find Gemma and Martin sitting on top of their bundles, down at the jetty.

I threw a rope and they helped me tie up and we loaded the last of the stores and our belongings on board. Then we were ready to sail. Home wasn't much but I felt a pang to leave it.

'We got the first aid kit and the medicine chest?' I asked.

Gemma held the medicine chest up for me to see.

'OK. Then let's go.'

So I cast the ropes off. Go, and be quick about it. That's

my way. I can't stand those farewells that linger – even when it's only rocks and stone you're saying goodbye to.

We'd only got a short way from the jetty when the most heart-rending, grief-stricken, pathetic noise rose into the sky. I looked to see who was crying. Gemma wouldn't – she liked to act tough. All her crying she did on her own, when no one was looking. It would have to be Martin, who didn't seem to have a boy's inhibitions about showing his feelings. But then, he'd never been told *not* to show them.

But it wasn't him either. It was someone else entirely. It was our sky-puss. Well, they're sky-riders to be more accurate. Those lazy scroungers do have the knack of inveigling their way into your affections; they curl up on your knee of an evening and start to purr, and you can't help but like them, even while admitting that they don't give a damn about you, and they're only in it for the titbits. They're the kind of pet whose philosophy is: You feed me, I love you. You stop feeding me, I go and love someone else. You get a few people like that as well.

Anyhow, there he was, on the jetty. We'd gone and forgotten about him and had been about to leave him behind. He wouldn't have starved. He just needed to get off his lazy backside and go and catch some sky-minnows. But no. That had too many similarities to a thing called hard work.

'Botcher!'

It was Martin who'd given him the name.

'Gran – we're not leaving him behind, are we?'

'He won't die, Martin. He is supposed to be a wild, foraging creature.'

'But he'll be lonely.'

'Oh – I guess.'

Gemma didn't comment, but I could see from her expression that she'd have left him behind easily.

'Here, Botcher! Here! Come on, boy! Here!'

He took a small run and leapt into the sky and then landed with a thump on the deck.

'Oooooow!'

He hadn't really hurt himself. He was just putting it on for sympathy, which Martin immediately gave him, picking him up and petting him and saying, 'Poor Botcher, did you bash your head? Never mind.'

'Just keep him from under my feet, Martin,' I said. 'You're looking after him for the duration of the trip, all right?' I had enough to worry about without a sky-puss on the make.

'And keep him out of my way too,' Gemma said sharply. She was having one of her sulky and sullen days. Maybe she was more apprehensive than she was letting on.

'Come on, Botcher. Let's go to the back.'

'It's called the stern. You should know that by now,' Gemma said.

'I know that,' Martin said. 'But Botcher doesn't.'

He took him to the stern of the boat and perched him on the rail. I looked back too, and saw the island behind us. It had started small anyway, and now it was getting smaller. I touched the tiller and opened the covers of the solar panels. I hoped my navigation was right. A compass is useless here. You've got magnetic fields coming at you from so many different directions at once that a compass needle would be spinning like a cork in a whirlpool. Charts are the only way to do it. Charts and landmarks and personal experience.

Had I been a religious type, I'd have said a prayer or two, round about then. But at one hundred and twenty years old, I was basically the doubting type. But, just to be on the safe side, I said a prayer anyway.

Anyhow, that's it from me. You don't want to hear the creak of old bones and the croak of old vocal cords any more, I'm sure. So someone else can take over the story. It's younger voices and fresher perspectives you want to hear. Those two there can divide it between them. Besides, I'm tired. I've told too many stories in my time. That's how it gets you in the end. You just want to sit back a spell, and let someone else do the talking.

So I'll pass you over to the younger generation, to the ones who can still get the greenstick fractures, and embarrass themselves without even trying. You've got to pass the baton over at some point; we all have; it's a relay, you see, that's the kind of race the human one is. Maybe somebody might even make it to the finishing post one day. But it sure won't be me. Though I've done my stretch of distance, and I ran it as best I could.

# 3

# first encounter

**MARTIN SPEAKING:**

That's my sister there by the mast, looking soulful, and that's my gran at the tiller – or, more strictly speaking, my great-great-grand-aunt (apparently). Her name's Peggy. Sometimes I call her Gran, sometimes I call her Peggy, sometimes I pretend I can't hear her, and sometimes I pretend she's not there. Sometimes I pretend I'm not there. Sometimes I pretend nothing's there. I just close my eyes and make it all go away, just like that.

Peggy says she's a hundred and twenty years old. But then she says a lot of things, and I don't believe half of them either. She might be a hundred and twenty years old. She might be a hundred and fifty years old. She looks it some days. And she sure isn't twenty-five any more. But I don't know. And that's the trouble – so Peggy says. Peggy says we don't know much at all, and that's why we need an education.

She says some people say that whoever increases knowledge

increases sorrow and that ignorance is bliss – but it isn't. She says ignorance is a pain in the butt. But I don't know if that's right either. Because I don't have any pains in my butt, and I'm supposed to be about as ignorant as you can get. According to Peggy. But my butt is an ache-free zone – except when Gemma kicked it once, but that's sisters for you. (And I waited my time and kicked hers right back too, as retaliation is best when it's unexpected.)

The problem, as I see it, is this: just say ignorance really is bliss . . . Well, the only way to find out if it is or not, is to get educated, and then you can make what Peggy calls 'an informed decision'. But if you then decide that ignorance is bliss after all, well, it's too late. Because by then you're already half educated. And you can't un-educate yourself or de-educate yourself, can you? So as far as being blissfully ignorant goes, you've had it. You're just going to be educated and miserable and longing for that far-off happy land, back when you didn't even realise that two and two made four. (I do know that much; we've covered basic arithmetic.)

So I just hope Peggy's not putting us wrong here. I just hope she knows what she's talking about this time. Because that's why we're sailing off into the blue and leaving everything familiar behind – to get an education. So it had better be a good one. As I was quite happy where I was. And if it turns out there's nothing in this education business, I'm going to be mighty peeved. Because I could be back there right now, on Peggy's island, fishing and mooching and doing what I always do, just being in the sun and letting the time go by, and no worries at all. No dramas.

'You're dreaming your life away, Martin, my boy,' Peggy would say to me, regular as meals coming round. But what if I was? Was there something wrong with that? Is there something wrong with dreaming? Can't a boy have a hobby and an interest? There's nothing wrong with dreaming. It keeps you out of trouble; it costs nothing; you can do it anywhere, and you don't need any special equipment: just your head and somewhere soft to rest it, and then your dreams.

'Dreamers are in for rude awakenings, Martin. Those are my words and you mark them.'

Yeah. Well, anyhow. So there we are and there we were. I'm not much on tenses. Peggy says I can get past, present and future all mixed up. But what's the difference? Yesterday, today, tomorrow – they're all much the same to me. Things happened or things are happening or things are going to happen. What does the when matter? It's the happening part that counts.

Some things I remember and some things I forget – it's like I wasn't even there, though I was, but I have this knack of being able not to pay any attention. Peggy says I could sleep through a war, and I probably could if it was a short one. But I wasn't asleep or daydreaming when we set off in Peggy's old boat that day. Because it was a big and memorable occasion. It isn't every day you leave home and go travelling. City Island, we were heading for. Peggy said it might take a few weeks to get there and it could be something of a rough crossing at times.

Peggy says a lot of things and you don't always know

whether to believe them. But sometimes she's right. Only too right. Sometimes she's bang on the nail.

OK. Well, it started off all right. There we were: me, Gemma, Peggy and Botcher the sky-puss – otherwise known as big, fat and useless. Well, maybe Botcher is good for something – making everybody else feel useful. He's good for your self-esteem. You only have to compare yourself to Botcher and you feel you're on a winning team and have big talents. But what he's best at is lounging and eating, though not necessarily in that order.

The sky was as blue as I'd ever seen it the day we set off. There was nobody to say goodbye to us except old Ben Harley, who is Peggy's nearest neighbour and is all white hair and whiskers and bits of red complexion and a nose that somebody maybe trod on by accident once upon a time, or swiped with a hammer.

We could see him in the distance, waving a goodbye by swinging an old pair of trousers back and forth. And we could hear him calling, 'Take it easy!' and, 'See you soon, Peggy!' And I reckoned that for all he and Peggy made out they didn't get on, in fact they did, and all this being crotchety towards each other was nothing but a show. I thought that he was going to miss her terrible and that she was sad to see him there waving his old trousers at her too.

Old Ben also shouted something that sounded like 'Bum foidge!'. When I asked Peggy what he was saying that for, she said he was saying, 'Bon voyage', which she said was one of the old world languages – French – and it meant

'Have a good journey', and that when we got to City Island and got educated we'd know all about stuff like that and be talking French like naturals. But Ben could just as well have said, 'Safe journey!' and then we'd have understood him straight away and wouldn't have needed to learn French. So I don't know why he didn't do that, unless he was showing off.

So that was the farewell party assembled to see us off – just old Ben Harley waving his trousers like a flag and shouting at us in French. And nobody else in the whole universe knew or cared that we were on our way to City Island to go to school and get educated and 'have a future' as Peggy called it.

But wouldn't we have had a future anyhow? I wondered. You didn't need to go to City Island to have a future. You could get one of those no matter where you went.

Soon old Ben was nothing but a shadow and Peggy's island was a distant stone. All there was around us was the blue of the sky and the specks that were faraway islands. There wasn't a cloud anywhere, not one, it was just blue, blue, burning blue – so blue it made your eyes ache and you longed for another colour, only there wasn't one, except the flash of a bright green sky-fish flying by, or the fluttering of an orange sky-clown, or the flabby white shape of a sail-fish, seeming to wander off in all directions at once.

'Martin!' Peggy shouted at me. She sounded annoyed.
'What?'
'You're the lookout, remember.'
'Huh?'

'Lookout. You're supposed to be looking out. You don't look like you're looking out to me. You look like you're just looking.'

'I was looking.'

'Yeah, well, you're supposed to be looking out!'

'Yes, dumb-head –' (That was Gemma butting in. Peggy never called you names or worked up to insults or was ever really rude to you. You need a sister to do all that.) 'You're supposed to be looking out on your side and I'm looking out on mine.'

'Well, I was looking out,' I said. Which was a lie, but I don't mind telling the occasional one. 'And even if I wasn't, there doesn't seem much to look out for.'

Peggy gave me one of her older-and-wiser looks.

'There never does until you see it,' she said.

'Well, what am I supposed to notice? What am I supposed to bring to anyone's attention?'

'Anything suspicious, anything dangerous, anything that looks like trouble.'

'There's her,' I said, pointing at Gemma. 'She looks like all of those. Especially the trouble.'

'Get lost, Martin.'

'Here? How? There's nowhere to get lost to.'

'Then try falling over the side –'

'OK, that's enough, you two. Just keep an eye out, Martin, all right? These are dangerous skies.'

'They look safe enough to me.'

'That's what's dangerous about them.'

'If you say so.'

'I do. So keep them peeled.'

So peeled is how I kept them. At least I did until they started closing. I saw nothing too interesting either, except a sky-shark, chasing its prey, and I thought to myself: Isn't that always the way of it, one thing wanting to eat another? And I've also noticed that the thing doing the eating is usually bigger than the thing being eaten. Not always, but most of the time. Unless it's bugs or sky-fleas, of course. But parasites eat you without necessarily killing you, whereas predators do the whole job in one.

And then, I guess, I just stopped peeling them and I maybe dozed off. When I opened up the eye hatches again, the sky was just the same bright blue, as blue as all monotony. Peggy's island had gone from view and old Ben waving his trousers was a snapshot in an album somewhere. I did wonder if I would ever see any of them again – Ben, the island, or the trousers.

But then I saw something else, looming up and looming large, and it was a little too late to avoid it.

'Land ho!' I shouted.

Peggy was down below. The boat was on autopilot. Gemma was trailing a fishing line over the rail at the back.

Peggy came up on deck.

'Land ho where?'

'Right there, Peg.'

I pointed to where we were heading. If I'd been keeping them alert and peeled like I was supposed to, we might have had time to take a little evasive action. But it was too late now. We were sailing along between two islands.

The port-side one looked barren and empty. The starboard side one was just as barren-looking but it was definitely inhabited. You could see that because there was a huge sign there, erected at the end of a jetty.

The sign had been hand-painted with what must have been a scraggy brush and a hand that was none too steady. It read THE TOLL TROLL IS:

And next to that there was a rack to hold another sign, which could be changed around as needed. The sign at that moment read IN. I assume the other side of it bore the word OUT.

But we were unlucky. The IN was up.

Next thing we saw was that slung between the two islands was a huge net. It could be lowered or raised by means of slackening or tightening a couple of ropes. We were unlucky with that too. The net was up and if we carried on sailing we'd have sailed right into it and have got tangled up like a shoal of fish in a sky-trawl.

'What the –?'

Peggy treated herself to some cursing.

'What's going on, Gran?' Gemma said.

'I don't know. But cut our speed or we'll be right into that damn net.'

Gemma reeled the sails in and Peggy shut the solar down.

And then the noise started. It was quite a racket. It sounded like someone taking a look at a sky-cat's intestines while the cat was still conscious. Botcher seemed to get the same idea, as he leapt up and scurried under a sail bag and tried to put his paws in his ears.

'For the love of –!'

The man on the shore was big and broad and he was wearing a skirt, or maybe it was a kilt of some kind, and he had large, muscled arms, covered in freckles and red hair. And he was playing some sort of bagpipes. But it was obvious, from the way he was playing them, that lesson number two in the Teach Yourself the Bagpipes correspondence course had not yet arrived.

After about thirty seconds, the ear torture ended. He stopped playing in order to swat at a whole swarm of insects that were bothering his beard. But no sooner had he swatted them away than they came back, like they couldn't live without him. So he gave up on the pipes and he bellowed at us, long and loud.

'Ahoy! You there!'

'What is it you want?' Peggy yelled back. 'We're just travelling. We're an old lady and two kids. We don't have anything.'

'Everyone's got something! And if you want to sail between my islands, you've got to pay.'

'Just told you, we don't have anything. Lower the net and let us pass.'

'No way, old timer. You pay the toll or you don't go nowhere.'

'"You don't go *anywhere*",' Peggy corrected him. 'You don't say "*you don't go nowhere*". That's a double negative. Watch your grammar. I'm trying to get these children to speak nicely, and bad examples of common usage don't help that.'

The big beardy one didn't answer her. He put his

bagpipes down, swatted away a few more of the insects that were bothering him, picked up a large harpoon that could have come off a sky-whaler, and fitted it into a gun fixed to the jetty.

'You pull to, or you get blasted.'

Peggy swore some of her swears again.

'I need this like a hole in the head, you red-bearded idiot!' she yelled at him.

'You don't pull over, you'll *get* a hole in the head,' he yelled back. 'This size.' And he pointed at the harpoon.

I saw Peggy look at me with what had to be reproach, but she didn't say anything. Maybe she knew I hadn't been keeping my eyes as peeled as I might have. Maybe the situation could have been avoided if I'd been a better lookout, but we couldn't avoid it now.

'OK,' she said. 'I'll bring the boat over.'

She turned the wheel and guided us towards the jetty.

The red-bearded, muscly one stood watching us come in, one hand on the harpoon gun, the other swatting the insects away. Maybe it was his beard they were in love with, or perhaps they liked to nestle in the undergrowth that thatched his arms. Either way they bothered him silly. It was no wonder he seemed in a bad mood.

We glided in to tie up at the jetty, where he stood waiting, big and fearsome and slightly unhinged-looking.

The Toll Troll was in, all right. And in a bad mood too. But then perhaps he was never in anything else.

# 4

# toll

**MARTIN STILL TALKING:**

Peggy, being so old, often doesn't seem so bothered about things that rightly ought to worry a person. I mean, I'm not a worrier. I've never really had anything to worry about – except for that time when we were small and we didn't have anyone and everybody kept calling us orphans (and usually poor ones too, as the words *orphans* and *poor* are kind of inseparable).

But even with a whole bunch of carefree years behind me, I was worried now. I'd never seen anything like this. The so-called, self-styled Toll Troll was even bigger close to than he'd seemed far away. He was immense. He was twice as tall as Peggy and as broad as a rock. He looked down on us like somebody contemplating his dinner and thinking that the helpings looked rather mingy. But Peggy just acted like she was the big muscly one, and he was the one-hundred-and-twenty-year-old sky-shrimp.

'Well?' she said, with a very sharp tone to her voice. 'And what do you want?'

'What do you think?' the huge man said. 'What does it look like?'

Only he didn't exactly say it like that, as he had a very odd accent, not like anything I'd heard before. He said it more like: 'Whit dee yee thunk? Whot daes it luuk lyke?' But his accent fluctuated. At first he was calm and clear, but then the more irritated he got, the more impenetrable it became.

'Why's he started talking funny, Peg?' I said. But I didn't get a proper answer. Peggy just glowered at me, Gemma kicked my shin, and the big guy kind of tensed up and started clenching his fists.

'Will ye tell yon brat tae hold his tongue before I rip it oot his mouth for him?' he said.

'Martin –'

But I'd heard.

'Good,' he said, when I clammed up.

'So what do you want?' Peggy said again.

'The toll. Whit else?' he said.

'Toll?'

'Aye.'

Peggy looked at him, up and sideways.

'And why should we pay you any toll?'

'Because I'm asking for it.'

'And what entitles you to ask?'

The big man looked around with a kind of false innocence, and then he slowly raised his big fist and he waved it under Peggy's nose.

'This,' he said. 'This does.'

'I see.'

'Good.'

'You're a crook then,' she told him.

The big man got indignant at that.

'I'm nae a cruk!' he said (his variable accent suddenly thick as cream). 'Ye want to use my airspace and sail between my islands, then ye have to pay.'

'Why?' Peggy said.

He stared at her, as if no one had asked him this before.

'To pay for all the maintenance,' he said.

'What maintenance?' she said.

He got angry again.

'The maintenance!' he repeated. 'Maintaining the highway and keeping it in good repair.'

'It's sky,' Peggy pointed out. 'You don't have to do anything to it. It's just there. So what are you maintaining exactly?'

The giant of a man thought about this for a moment; he stood winding bits of his straggly red beard around his fingers, then said:

'I'm keeping the sky clean and free from debris.'

And that was when I heard Peggy mutter something that sounded like *bullsh*— But I'm not supposed to know expressions like that, let alone use them.

The man looked down at her. The insects went on swarming around his head, like some kind of a halo. Some of the midges were even nibbling at his hairy legs, which poked out like tree trunks from his kilt. I wondered if maybe the insects had driven him mad.

'No toll,' he said, 'no go.'

'Well, that's too bad,' Peggy said, 'because we've nothing to give you.'

The man sneered.

'Everyone's got something,' he said.

'I'm an old woman with two children; we've no money and just enough food and water to last the journey. We're heading for City Island so they can go to school and get an education. And that's it.'

'Bairns!' the man said. 'Nothing but trouble and nothing but expense. That's bairns.'

Peggy sat down on the jetty. The giant looked down at her with outraged surprise.

'What are you doing?' he said. 'What do you think you're doing?'

'Sitting down,' Peggy said. 'I get the arthritis.'

'She gets the arthritis,' Gemma said, backing her up. 'And she can't be on her feet too long without a break.'

'Break?' the giant of a man said, speckles of froth appearing on his lips and on the fringes of his beard. 'I'll give you a break. I'll break your necks. I'll break your skulls open with the hilt of my claymore –' And he indicated a long-bladed, heavy-handled sword, covered in rust, that stood stuck in the ground nearby.

His indignation rose like steam until it was all but puffing out of his ears.

'You dinnae sit down when the Toll Troll's talking. You quake in fear, that's what you do. You quake and tremble and beg for mercy. That's the style you need. I've never been so bloody insulted!'

'No swearing in front of the children, if you wouldn't mind,' Peggy said.

'Nae swearing? Nae swearing! I'll give you swearing –'

But Peggy just reached out and said, 'I wonder if you'd mind giving me a hand up now. I can't sit down too long either or I start getting the cramps.'

'She gets cramps,' Gemma explained, 'as well as the arthritis. She's a hundred and twenty, you see, and not as young as –'

'Will ye all shut up!' the man said. 'All of ye. Just shut up and let me think.'

While he was thinking, I got curious. Peggy says curiosity is my trouble, but I can't help it. These questions just form in my mind, and when they do, I have to ask them, as I like to find things out.

'Excuse me,' I said. 'Mister Troll –'

His eyebrows moved like a couple of those sun caterpillars you sometimes see on the rocks – the furry, poisonous ones that'll kill you if you brush against them.

'Whit did you just say?' He looked at Peggy. 'Whit did he just say? I thought yon brat was supposed to be keeping his teeth together and his mooth shut.'

'I was just wondering, Mister Troll,' I persisted, 'if you had another name. Like, a real name. And what it was.'

The eyebrows went on working. I really did think for a moment that they might come off and attack me. But then they came to rest and they arched into a look of, well, perplexity, I guess.

'Ma name?' He turned to Peggy. 'No one's ever asked me ma name. And I've robbed – that is, I've needed to take toll money from – hundreds, no, thousands who've passed by here. And no one's ever asked me ma name.'

Peggy just looked at him and gave him one of her old smiles. Her smiles are full of wrinkles and crows' feet and leathery skin and a hundred and twenty years of living.

'Out of the mouths of babes and children,' she said.

'Well, I'm nae telling you ma name!' the Troll said. And he sounded a bit peevish, like *he* was the spoilt brat – instead of a massive man with a sword and bagpipes and a kilt and a big chip on his shoulder from somewhere.

'My name's Peggy. This is Gemma. This is Martin. So there. We're introduced.'

'Well – then –' It was plainly an effort for him to let the words come out. 'Then ma name – might be – though I'm no saying it is – but it might be – Angus.'

'That's a nice name,' Peggy said. 'Angus. Very nice.'

One of the caterpillars came back into action and it arched itself up into a quizzical sort of shape.

'Are ye trying to be funny?'

'No. Not at all.'

But then the brief thaw turned to ice again.

'It makes nae difference!' he boomed. And he went and yanked the claymore out of the ground. It was a huge sword. It took both of his hands to lift it. 'Makes nae difference what anyone's called. You have to pay the toll or you don't go any further.'

And then he swirled the sword around his head. But whether it was to frighten and intimidate us, or whether it was to try and get rid of the insects that were tormenting him was hard to know.

Something puzzled me then. Why *did* the insects bother him? They weren't bothering me, or Gemma, or Peggy. The just seemed to like eating him. They left us alone completely.

I looked past him. The island wasn't that large and it looked mostly barren. There was a vapour compressor next to a small stone house and behind the house a greenhouse, where he must have grown a few vegetables to supplement a diet of sky-fish – as I couldn't see what else he might have lived on. A sign on the door of the house read Bonny Banks. There was a small outside lavatory too, and that had a door-sign reading Bonny Braes.

To the right of the house, at a short distance, were some small mounds of stones – cairns, I think they are called. I'm sure that's what Peggy told me once. But I might have been wrong.

'I may have to sit down a moment again,' Peggy said. 'I get dizzy if I'm up on my feet too long. I suffer with the poor circulation.'

'She suffers with the poor circulation,' Gemma said, backing her up again. 'Along with the arthritis and the cramps.'

'And then there's the gout,' Peggy said.

'And the gout,' Gemma said.

'But we'll not go into that right now.'

'We'll leave it for now,' Gemma said. 'It's not serious gout. Mostly twinges. I don't suppose you'd have a chair, would you? For Gran to sit on?'

Angus lowered his claymore and stood there open-mouthed.

'A chair? A chair!'

'If you've got one?'

He raised the claymore and pressed the point of it right into Gemma's neck. She stiffened.

'Leave her alone,' Peggy said.

So he did. He stuck the point into Peggy's neck instead.

'You pay, or you pay,' he said. 'You pay the toll, or you pay the troll. Your money or –' Then he struck a pose of what's-the-word-I'm-trying-to-think-of? – 'Oh aye. Your money, or your life. That's how it goes, isn't it?'

'Just told you,' Peggy said, 'don't have any money. Haven't had any money since I was eighty-three.'

'Blew it all, did you?' Angus said in disgust. 'Typical. Didn't think of making any provision for your old age.'

'And as for life, I don't have much of that left either.'

'Maybe you don't – but *they* do.'

'What are you going to spend money on here, anyway?' Peggy demanded. 'Where are the shops?' She moved her arms to indicate the empty islands and the vast, empty space beyond. And the gesture encompassed everything – the giant's isolation, his loneliness, the pointlessness of his demands and the uselessness of money to him. Why did he want it? What was it for?

'I'm making provision,' he said. 'It's nae for me. I'm making provision for the wife and bairns.'

And he swatted so violently at the midges around his head that he almost decapitated himself with his sword – which would have solved our problems nicely if he had.

Peggy looked at me and she looked at Gemma; she looked sad, and old. She didn't look frightened at all, just ever so weary.

'Wife and bairns?' she said.

'That's right,' Angus said. 'It's not for me. It's the wife and bairns.'

And then Peggy asked him a question, though I'm sure she already knew the answer, just as I did, and Gemma maybe did too.

'And where are they? The wife and – the bairns?'

'They're right there looking at you!' the giant said. 'Do you not have the eyes to see? That's Colin there, and that's Nancy, and that's Fiona herself, taking care of them.'

I was kind of afraid to look. But really, I'd already seen. My eyes followed his raised hand and his pointing finger. And I saw – just as I knew I would – the three heaps of stones, the three little cairns, the mounds of pebbles and rocks.

'That's them right there,' he said. 'They'd come over and talk, but they're busy. But they're relying, see. They're relying on me to provide. They'll be wanting to go to school one day and get an education. There's none to be

41

had round here. City Island, see. That's where they'll be going, soon as they're the right age. So I'm saving up – for books and such, and uniforms and all that. So there's no choice about it. You have to pay the toll.'

And instead of protesting or getting angry or feisty or sarcastic like she could be, Peggy just looked really sad, and she reached out to him and she said, 'We'd love to give something to help the children, Angus. We'd love to do that.'

And he just looked at her, just looked, and the big, rusty claymore fell from his hands with a clatter, and Peggy took a step forward and she took his great, huge hand in hers. His hand made two of hers, easily.

'You poor man,' she said. 'You poor man.'

And the great giant of an Angus didn't say a word; he just let Peggy hold his hand in hers, and a large tear, the size of a raindrop, rolled from his eye and down along his cheek and disappeared into his bushy red beard.

'Will you take payment in kind?' Peggy said.

'What kind?' he said gruffly.

'Martin,' Peggy said. 'Go to the boat and fetch one of the bottles that Ben Harley gave me.'

'You mean the private stash?' I said. 'But I thought you said it was lethal. I thought you said you should never –'

'Just get it,' she said. 'And stop asking questions for once.'

'But I thought you said asking questions was good, and that when we get to City Island we have to ask nothing but questions, as if you don't ask questions you never learn, and then –'

'Another time, Martin. Just bring a bottle of Ben Harley's private stash.'

'All right.'

'And hurry up too, Martin.'

'All right, Gemma. Since when were you in charge –?'

I went to get what Peggy wanted from the boat.

'Kids, eh?' I heard Angus say behind me. 'Brother and sister, often arguing. Mine are the same. But they love each other underneath. Mine are the same,' he repeated. 'Just the same –'

I found one of Ben Harley's bottles of private stash and returned to the jetty.

'Open it and give it to Mr Angus,' Peggy said.

I pulled the stopper out of the bottle neck. That familiar foul smell hit me. Old Ben Harley's home-made private stash was disgusting. The smell soon wore off though, once the air got at it.

I knew why she was giving it to Angus. And I knew now why the midges weren't bothering us.

'There. That's our toll paid.'

Peggy put the bottle into Angus's hand. He sniffed at it.

'It's poison.'

'No, just smells like it. I wouldn't drink it though. It's got better uses. Just dab some on your beard.'

He did. Then he re-corked the bottle and set it down.

'Well? Now what?'

'Well, look at yourself.'

'How can I look at myself,' Angus said, 'when there's nae mirror? There's been nae mirror for years.'

'Evidently . . .' Peggy muttered.

'Then what's this stuff do?'

'Haven't you noticed?'

It took him a few more seconds. Then a smile spread across his face.

'The midges!' he said. 'They're leaving me alone! They've tormented me every minute of the day since I can't remember! They're leaving me alone!'

'And it'll last a long time too,' Peggy said. 'Especially if you're not big on washing.'

'Don't have the water to spare,' Angus said. 'Not that that means I don't maintain standards. Always been big on personal hygiene. A bath every three or four months, whether I need it or not.'

'I'm pleased to hear it,' Peggy said. 'Then that bottle there should last you years. You just need a dab and they'll keep their distance and not bother you again.'

'It's wonderful,' Angus said. 'It's like someone turned the misery off.'

'Is that us quits then?' Peggy said. 'Have we paid the toll?'

'More than paid it,' Angus said. 'But I don't have any change.'

'We're not expecting any,' Peggy said. 'Just happy to help. Aren't we?'

'Yes, Gran,' Gemma agreed.

'Very happy,' I said.

'Then I'll let you get on your way,' the Troll said – and he wasn't really such a troll now. He was just another person, a rather large and frightening one, but essentially just like us.

'We'll do that then,' Peggy said. 'Gemma, Martin –'

'Goodbye, Angus,' Gemma said.

'What a pretty wee girl,' Angus said to Peggy. 'I compliment you on your granddaughter. She's just like my Nancy. So young, and full of life – and the young man here, reminds me of my Colin . . .' And then his voice trailed away.

'A pleasure to meet you, Mr Angus,' I said.

'A pleasure to meet you all. And thank you for the . . . thanks.'

'Not at all. If you're ready then –'

Peggy led us aboard. Angus helped us untie and he stood watching from the jetty as we uncovered the solar panels and unfurled the wind sails.

He undid the lines that held up the net blocking our way; the net sank down and we were free to leave.

'Sail safely now,' he said. 'Mind how you go. There's some weird people about,' he said. 'You want to be careful.'

'It's just straight on, isn't it?' Peggy said.

'That's the way. Empty sky for about fifty kilometres, and then you'll see the Isle of Ignorance.'

'We'll see the what?'

We were already sailing and his voice was lost on the wind.

'Ignorance. You'll see it. But keep going.'

And he waved, and we moved on.

I looked back. We could just see him changing the sign by the jetty.

It now read THE TOLL TROLL IS: OUT.

And he was reeling the net in, and the way was now clear. And there was no longer a swarm of angry midges around his head, and he somehow looked less angry too.

The last we saw of him, he was standing by the three stone mounds, as if engaging them in conversation. But what he was saying we could only imagine, or fail to imagine. For who knows what is really in another person's heart? That was what Peggy told me.

'So what did we learn back there?' she said, once we had put a good distance between Angus and ourselves.

'I don't know, Peggy,' I said. 'Eh . . . we learned that his real name was Angus?'

'What else?'

'Eh . . . I don't know.'

'Gemma?'

'Plenty,' Gemma said.

'Tell me what you learned,' Peggy said.

'Not to judge people on first appearances. That angry people are often upset and in pain inside. That you never really know about anyone, that your first impressions can be completely wrong. And that underneath everything we all have a lot in common, and we all suffer in the same way, and can all be happy in the same way.'

Peggy smiled.

'That's right.' She nodded. 'That's right.'

It was all a bit above my head, to be honest. All I felt

I'd learned was that the troll's name was Angus. But there you are.

Taking advantage of the situation though, I said, 'Peggy – if we've already learned so much about life, do we *have* to go to City Island? Couldn't we just turn around and go back home?'

'Martin,' she said. 'You can learn about life anywhere. But if you want to learn about physics, chemistry, history, geography, economics, languages, algebra and quadratic equations, then you have to go to school.'

'I don't know that I do want to learn about quadratic equations,' I said. 'I don't know what they are but I can't say I like the sound of them.'

'You'll love them,' she said. 'Once you get started.'

But I wasn't so sure about that. I had this sense of vague unease. There was something about quadratic equations that didn't sound very inviting.

# 5
# cooking

**GEMMA SPEAKING NOW. HER TURN:**

Peggy said from the off that we had to get Martin to do the cooking. She said, back in the very old days, it was always girls who got stuck with the cooking, but Martin wasn't going to know that, so we'd stick him with the cooking instead, right from the start.

'How is he going to know any different?' Peggy had said. After all, there were just the three of us. It wasn't as if he was going to pick up bad habits from elsewhere. The only other male of the species (as Peggy called them) within visiting distance was old Ben Harley. And he was stuck with the cooking too, and as far as he was concerned, it was cook or die. For who else was going to do it, as he was on his ownsome?

When I say we stuck Martin with the cooking, that's not strictly as bad as it sounds. All we did was get him to do his share. So that was accepted. We all had to help. Sometimes it was washing-up; sometimes it was cooking; sometimes it was keeping the place clean. You always got stuck with something. But when everyone else is getting stuck with something too, you don't mind. It's when you're stuck with everything and everyone else is stuck with nothing – like Cinderella, who Peggy told us about – that's when you feel aggrieved. It's seeing those ugly sisters with their feet up on the coffee table and their bums on the sofa cushions all day long that gets you riled.

All the stories we know come from Peggy – the Cinderellas and so forth. She's got plenty that she can recite off by heart and there were books in the house, but not many, as they were hard to come by. There's no visiting library boat out where Peggy lived; the only other literature you get there is what's written in the clouds, or the future that's scrawled across the palm of your hand – if you believe in that kind of thing, and I don't, though I don't mind pretending for fun.

It's another of the reasons why we have to go to City Island and meet new people. Peggy says she's got no more stories left and she's told us them all. She's all storied out. She says there's plenty more out there, but she doesn't know or can't remember them no more. Or rather – any more. I've got to remember that. It's grammar. We're not supposed to say *no more* no more. We've got to say *any more* from now on.

Peggy says there's books out there like you'll never see the end of. She says there's so many that no one could ever read them all, not even if they made it their life's work and dedication. Seems hard to imagine to me. I can't even picture that many books, not like walls and walls of them, going on forever, but Peggy says they've got books in City Island like fish in the sky.

And then there's boys. Peggy says they've got almost as many boys as books and you could never get to the end of all of them either. She says it's time I met some, but I don't know. I mean, Martin's a boy and so what? But Peggy says a boy's not like a brother. She says a boy who's not a brother is a completely separate thing and an entirely different kettle of fish. So I had to ask her what a kettle of fish was, and why you'd be cooking fish in a kettle. But she said it was just an expression, and that was all the kind of thing we'd get the hang of once we arrived at City Island.

I'm just hoping all this education is going to be one bit as marvellous as Peggy's making out it is. I've been disappointed before. She said that eating sky-oysters was a real treat when you can get them. But when we did find them, I thought they were disgusting and tasted like slime with extra slime added. So I hope that finally going to school isn't going to be like that.

The expression is always *finally* going to school with Peggy. Other kids, I reckon, just go to school. But not us, we *finally* go to school, like we're the last to arrive or something.

Anyway, I just hope she's right and that it is going to be something special and we're not going all this way for nothing. Though I am interested in seeing what all the fuss over boys is about. Not that I'm fussed or making a fuss. It's Peggy who's gone on about them. She just says we gotta go out into the world and grow up normal. She says growing up on our ownsome with a batty old woman – which is what she calls herself and we've ended up stopping arguing and contradicting with her as she seems kind of proud of being batty, to say the truth – but she says that growing up with a batty old woman like her isn't good for two kids. She says it's all right when you're little but that we aren't so little any more, especially me. She says (when he's out of hearing distance) that maybe Martin still is a little bit little but that I'm not and that I am growing up apace.

That's the kind of word she uses sometimes. I like that expression, that you are growing up *apace*. It just means quick but it somehow sounds better. Peggy says there's all kinds of words like that, ones that are plain and simple, and other ones that have poetry in them.

Anyhow, Martin doesn't really remember. Not like I do. It's all buried deep down in the underground for him; he was so young and small when our parents were lost. But when you lose your mum and dad, it's like the ground has gone and you're falling, falling, falling, all the way down into the sun. And plenty of times that was what I wished would happen and it would be the better and the easier way. I even said so to Peggy, when she found me crying once, that sometimes life feels so bad that you'd rather not live it, and you miss people so much you'd rather be with them than go on living. She said that was true and she could understand that, but we have to go on. And when I asked why, she said what about Martin, what would Martin do, as I was all he had left now, and he was all I had too.

And when you think about that, it's right I guess, and sometimes you don't go on because you really want to, you go on for someone else's sake. And when you do, after a while, the happiness slowly comes back into you, and you want to be alive again, just for the feeling of it, because it's nice and you might even be happy – not that you'll ever forget. But I don't think he remembers or knows any of that. That's the difference a couple of years makes. It can make all the difference sometimes, just being a little bit older.

Not that I'm getting all sentimental and dewy-eyed (that's another of Peggy's expressions; I sound like her sometimes and have been *unduly influenced* by her, which is another of her sayings). I mean, he's my brother and all that but I have hated his guts on occasions and he can still really get on my nerves and I have even wished he would drop dead. But Peggy says that's normal and when we get to City Island we'll meet other girls and boys who have had similar experiences. So all because you feel like murdering your brother occasionally, there's no call to feel bad about it, as that's what people do.

Oh well. I don't know. I don't know if I really want to go to school or what I want. Life's been so strange and sometimes so sweet and peaceful. It's been just us for years and years, me and Martin and Peggy, and old Ben Harley across the way, making sure to come over for birthdays and other celebrations, always bringing you a small present though nothing special, just something he'd carved out of a piece of driftwood or a polished stone or a bracelet made of sky-clam shells.

And now here we are, going out into the world, and we've only gone a short way and it already seems full of crazies – at least if Angus the self-styled Toll Troll is anything to go by. If he's what you meet when you go looking for an education then I can see the benefits of ignorance all right.

But anyway, I'm talking on again. Peggy says it's lack of company that keeps me talking, as I don't have anyone around me with something new to say that I haven't heard before, so I just go on talking like I'm on overdrive. Stream of consciousness, she calls it. She says I'll find out what that means when –

Yeah. You've got it. When we arrive at City Island and get an education.

I promise I won't mention that again. No, well, I don't exactly guarantee – but I promise I'll try. Do my best. Peggy says that's all you can do.

Anyhow again. We left big Angus behind us and we sailed on. Peggy's boat wasn't huge, but it was decent-sized. It had six berths down below and you could easily sleep another six or more on deck – which was where I liked to sleep most of the time. It's cooler there and nicer, as long as the bugs don't bite. When you get a midge bloom

53

though, you've got to take cover or they'll eat you right down to the pimples. The only thing that will keep them off is an application of old Ben Harley's private stash. That repels most living things, so Peggy says.

There are other hazards to sleeping on deck too, of course. You can wake up and find a couple of sky-fish nibbling at your feet. They like to eat the dead skin off you, which is OK for a quick pedicure. The trouble is, they don't know when to stop and when they run out of dead skin, they'll start in on the bits of you that are living. But you always wake up before they get to eat much of you. And you can always keep your sandals on.

The other thing you need to sleep on deck is something to cover your eyes as it's always daylight up there. I made myself a sleep mask out of an old piece of cloth. Martin made himself one too. Peggy said boys should be able to sew as well and she showed us both how. She said the days when girls got stuck with the sewing were long gone and she wasn't letting them come back without a struggle.

So we left old, sad, mad, not-so-bad Angus behind us, and Peggy checked the charts and said we were sailing right, and had our bearings accurate, and so on we went.

It was a lazy sort of progress, as Peggy's old boat was never built for speed; it's too chubby round the middle and it sits in the air like a fat old sky-whale, solid and slow and unsinkable-looking. If it had a steam engine it would chug along, but it doesn't, so it kind of chugs but without the chugging, if you get what I mean.

There wasn't a whole lot by way of scenery at the

beginning of our journey. We weren't in an interesting part of the system and were still days and days from the Main Drift. It was all little islands and floating rocks and bits of junk and debris passing by on the solar wind. And there were sky-fish and jellies and all the usual, and here and there some sky-crabs clinging on, with more legs than a creature could ever reasonably have a use for, to the undersides of the islands.

'Well, I don't know about you two, but I'm getting hungry,' Peggy announced in her usual way. 'Whose turn is it?'

Well, it was Martin's. And he was perfectly happy to get on with it.

'I'll throw a line over the side,' he said. 'See what I get.'

Because that was about all there was to eat: sky-fish. I mean, I've heard Peggy say about people who lived on nothing but vegetables and would never eat a fish not even to save their lives. But there's not a great deal of choice here. It's fish or hungry. Sure, we had a few veg and things on board that came from Peggy's greenhouse, and there were some pots along the deck with a few herbs and basics growing in them, but it would never have kept you going. So it was fish, fish, and sometimes, for a change, fish, when you were travelling. You couldn't change the meal, just the way it was cooked.

So Martin threw a couple of lines over and I did the same while Peggy lay down in her hammock on the deck, slung between the mast and a rigging line, as she said (as ever) that she was old bones and had to take it easy in the afternoons so as to ward off the arthritis and cramps.

It didn't take us long to wind in a couple of sky-fish and soon we had ingredients aplenty. (Which is a word a little like *apace*.)

'That should do it, Martin,' I said. But no. He wouldn't listen.

'Couple more,' he said. 'Don't have enough yet.'

Well, the fact is, when it comes to the cooking, that Martin has one problem – he always makes too much. He can cook all right. For his age he's a pretty fine chef. But his eyes are bigger than his stomach, and my stomach, and Peggy's stomach. So there's always leftovers and it's always getting wasted and ends up going off or getting thrown away.

Now, back on Peggy's island, that didn't matter. All the waste went into the composter and she'd use it for growing her fruit and veg. But out here in the middle of the sky, there was nowhere for it to go except over the side. Which shouldn't have been a problem – you might think. But you'd think wrong, just like we did. And wrong thinking brings consequences, every time.

# 6

# sky-shark

**GEMMA CONTINUES:**

I left him to it. That's the rule. When you're stuck with the cooking you get on with it and no interference. There's not really the space in the galley for two cooks anyway, and besides, according to Peggy, they spoil the broth. Although, on the other side of the coin, two heads are better than one and many hands make light work. Peggy says it doesn't matter what any one proverb says, there's always another to contradict it. She says proverbs are like people and their opinions – they seldom agree with each other.

So Martin got on with the sky-fish – all the gutting and scraping and the rest – while I checked the sails and the course we were taking. It looked OK so I lay in the other hammock up on deck and watched the blue sky overhead, and when some clouds appeared I tried to work out what they looked like. But most of them just looked like clouds, and I couldn't decide if it was they who lacked the imagination or me.

I must have dozed off, for when I woke again it was to the odour of cooking rising up from the galley and it didn't smell bad either. Then Martin appeared, shouting, 'It's ready!' and carrying a pot, and some bowls and cutlery, so we could eat up on deck.

'Smells good, Martin,' Peggy said, and she waved at me to help her out of her hammock, as she had trouble doing that on her own, due to the old bones situation.

I got her up and then went and poured us a glass of water each from storage. We were still good for water and had enough for a long while yet. Then we sat down to eat. It was sky-fish, oven-baked, with herbs and greens and rice and seasoning. But never mind three, there was enough for six.

'Martin –'

'Better too much than not enough.'

'It's all going to be wasted.'

'I'll feed it to the fish. They like leftovers.'

'I guess.'

There was no pudding. You don't get much pudding here. You can go weeks and months without pudding. Peggy said that when we got to City Island it would be pudding every day. But I wasn't bothered. You don't miss what you never have. I told Peggy that as far as I was concerned, pudding was just theoretical and academic – which was another of her sayings, and which my using made her smile. Maybe I didn't use it right but she didn't correct me, just smiled.

As Martin had been stuck with the cooking I was stuck with the washing-up. Peggy offered to do it, as she believes in democracy, to which age is no barrier. But I said no, I would do it, as she was stuck with us and that was worse than the dishes. Which made her smile again. And she said no, she wasn't stuck with us, but that the years she'd had us had been among the best.

And that was the first time it crossed my mind that when we got to City Island to begin a new life, Peggy wouldn't be starting one with us. She would be going back to her island, all on her own, and she might be lonely. And even old Ben Harley across the divide wouldn't keep that loneliness away, as we'd been with her every moment of our lives for such a long time, and suddenly we wouldn't be there any more.

I felt sad and sorry then. It's not nice to be old and lonely – or young and lonely either, come to that. And I thought that I would miss her. Or worse, I wouldn't, as I'd have this new exciting life on City Island with proper boys (not just brothers) around the place, who might be distracting, and I'd never think of Peggy at all – which would be awful, after everything she'd done.

There'd be other girls there too, my own age, who might be my friends, as I'd never even *seen* another girl, not for a long time, let alone made a friend of one. Martin and I hadn't seen another living boy or girl for years.

I tried to put all that out of my mind. But before I did, I vowed I wouldn't forget Peggy, and I'd not let her be lonely, if I could prevent it somehow.

I gathered up the dirty plates and bowls.

'What do you want to do with all these leftovers, Martin?'

'I'm going to feed them to the sky-fish.'

So I handed him the pot and he scraped it out over the side.

Which was a big mistake.

See, you shouldn't feed the sky-fish.

Oh, you can feed them raw titbits, that's fine, that's no problem at all. But cooked – that's different.

I suppose that sky-fish are kind of cannibals really. If a fish eats a fish then it's eating its own species – which makes it a cannibal, right? Fish are predators. But when they eat each other, they eat each other raw. They don't get the griddle out, or put the oven on to warm up, as they leaf through the recipe books.

The little sky-fish are no problem when you throw them scraps, raw or cooked. They turn up in their reeling shoals and gulp down what you've tossed over the side. Then they maybe hang around a while to see if there's any more forthcoming, and when there isn't, they scoot off.

It's the bigger fish that are the trouble. Not that we knew that then. Maybe Peggy did, and she forgot to tell us. But if a big fish gets the taste for cooked food, it doesn't go away. It hangs around wanting more. And there's one fish in particular that's very fond of a little variety to its diet. It's the sky-shark. And of all the varieties of sky-shark, the worst is the Great Blue. It's got teeth like chisels, and jaws that can snap a mast in half.

But we weren't thinking of anything like that as Martin scraped the cooked leftovers out of the boat and let them float away, as the little sky-fish got the scent of them and gave chase.

I carried the plates and bowls down below and got on with the washing-up. I took my time and did a thorough job and put everything back in its place – as you have to keep a boat shipshape or everything'll be under your feet.

I was just admiring my handiwork and thinking how tidy the galley looked, when the boat suddenly rocked, as if we'd bashed into a jetty, or collided with some massive piece of driftwood.

'What the –! Martin! What are you *doing* up there?'

When there's trouble, and when you have a younger brother, your first instinct is to assume that he's the one responsible for it. And you're generally right.

'Martin! What have you *done*?'

I hurried out of the galley and clambered up on deck. The first thing I saw was Martin, standing like he'd been turned to stone; the second thing I saw was Peggy, staring like she'd never seen anything to compare to this before, not in all her one hundred and twenty years.

The third thing I saw was a creature about half the size of the boat, hovering no more than a couple of metres above the deck; its side-fins pulsating like the wings of some gigantic hummingbird. It had the blackest, beadiest eyes I had ever seen, and from its open mouth dripped beads of what had to be saliva, falling from teeth that had tips like razors and were the size of swords.

'What the – what is *that*?'

Well, I knew what it was, but it wasn't a definition I was after, more a reason for its being there.

'Martin –'

'I wouldn't come any nearer if I were you, Gemma . . .'

'Peggy . . . ?'

'Gemma – just move really slowly and get over towards the mast and see if you can pick up that boathook – but slowly . . .'

'OK . . . I . . .'

I started to move, and *very* slowly.

'What does it want?' I said.

'It wants more,' Martin said. 'I think. More leftovers.'

'So give it some and it might go away.'

'There aren't any.'

I was halfway across the deck. The two black beads of those eyes swivelled towards me.

'Don't move, Gemma. Just stop a while.'

Which wasn't easy, as my every instinct was to run. Not that there was anywhere to run to.

'When it realises there's no more leftovers, it might go,' I said, with a sort of hopeful naivety.

'I don't think so, Gem,' Peggy said. 'I think it's got the taste now.'

'Taste for what?'

'Warm flesh,' Peggy said.

I felt my heart thudding in my chest, and try as I did, somehow I just couldn't swallow. My mouth filled with saliva. I'd soon be dribbling, like a sky-shark, if I wasn't careful. That, or I'd be its dinner.

There's always a problem with 'right here'. You ever noticed that? Other places suddenly seem to have their unsurpassable advantages, and where you're actually at right now doesn't look so great any more.

'Gemma ... don't worry ... just don't move quickly ...'

Peggy didn't need to say that. I wasn't going anywhere.

'Just wait ...'

I did.

In the old world – so Peggy told us once – the planet was mainly water. Bits of land, but mostly water, and the fish were happy to stay in the sea. They swam under you or alongside you. But they couldn't come out of the ocean and swim right next to you or swoop down on you from above, or decide to follow you home. I could now see all the pluses of a place like that.

'Wait and see what it's going to do ...'

The Great Blue hovered there, fins beating. It flicked its tail and spun around. If I'd reached up, I could have touched it, leathery skin and all. It could move so fast it was like it hadn't moved at all, just changed position by willpower alone.

'Don't bother it and it might go ...'

I had the boathook in both hands now. I'd slowly reached out and got it. But those teeth could have crunched it into pieces. Peggy was standing as still as a rock, and Martin was staring at the Great Blue, watching the balls of saliva drip from its gaping mouth and splash onto the deck, landing with a kind of sizzle, as if they were acid.

'It'll go. Just leave it and it'll go . . .' he said.

It might have done too, if it hadn't been for your friend and mine. He'd been down below sniffing around in the galley, looking for titbits, but now here he came, up the steps, fat-faced, lazy-eyed, good – as usual – for nothing. Botcher. Botcher the sky-cat. A nice, warm-blooded snack.

He saw the sky-shark hovering two metres above him, froze solid, and then decided he needed the toilet. He had my sympathy. I felt the same.

'Botcher, not on the . . .' Peggy began, but she trailed off.

Funny how things that don't really matter – given the circumstances – still seem to matter somehow. Standards, Peggy was fond of saying, have to be maintained.

The Great Blue saw him. Fat, friendly-looking sky-puss. Good old Botcher. A nice little lap-warmer and a tasty morsel too.

The sky-shark's eyes appeared to work independently of each other. One swivelled to look down at Botcher; the other kept on staring directly at me.

'Gem . . . he's going to eat Botcher . . .'

To be honest, in some ways, it seemed like a sacrifice worth making. If it would eat Botcher and go away . . . well, you can always get another fat, useless sky-puss without any trouble. But then, we'd had him for years, and it may have

64

been a bit of a strange-shaped family, but he was a part of it, in his bone-idle way.

'One of the eyes, Gemma . . .'

I'd known that instinctively. But just the thought of it turned me over. The stomach, the throat, the chest – that I could do. But it had to be something that would stop it in its tracks.

The Great Blue flipped a fin and spun round again. It angled in for the kill, tail up, nose down. Botcher sat looking at it. You might not believe that a sky-cat could sob, but he did. He was just a big ball of absolute terror.

Then the Great Blue opened its mouth wider, ready for the big, swallow-whole bite. You could see all its teeth, both sets of them, and sharp as knives.

'Gemma . . .'

I knew I had to do it and I wanted to do it with my eyes closed. But that would have been no good as I might have missed. So just as the Great Blue went in for the kill, I stabbed upwards with the boathook, thrusting it in with all my strength.

'Oh, that is . . . revolting!'

I jumped back. Botcher ran. I could hear Martin throwing up. The Great Blue crashed to the deck and began writhing. Peggy was over next to me then, taking the boathook and telling me to get out of the way. She stuck the hook in again, aiming for its heart. For an old lady she was stringy but strong. She pulled the boathook out again and rammed it in once more, as if she and sky-sharks had an old grievance, and she was getting her own back for past losses, and finally settling old scores.

The sky-shark let out the most awful gasp, fighting for breath and survival. It thrashed over the deck, its huge body crushing and knocking things aside. Then it flapped its fins and managed to get briefly back into the air, like it might manage to escape. But its strength gave out and it crashed again onto the boat, with a horrendous screech coming from it. There was the sound of things breaking as it twisted around on deck, then it finally stopped moving, and at last it was still and quiet, and just lay there in a pool of blood, on top of the now-smashed solar panels.

'Is it dead?'

Martin approached it.

'Just wait, Martin.'

Peggy stood, boathook in hand. She gave the shark a couple of prods.

'It's OK. It's gone.'

Botcher ventured near. All bravery and swagger now, as if he'd killed the sky-shark himself. But when those huge jaws twitched again, in the throes of death, he was off like a harpoon to the far end of the boat.

'What are we going to do with it?' Martin said. 'And the stink!' He was right. It didn't smell too good. 'And what's *that*?'

Sky-lice were crawling away from the dead shark.

'Rats,' Peggy said. 'Deserting the sinking ship.'

She stamped on them.

'And we don't want them either.'

'But what are we going to do with it?' Martin said.

'Throw it overboard.'

'How? I mean, look at its teeth.' Then he got covetous. 'Can I pull one out? As a souvenir?'

'Martin! Stay away.'

'Only looking.'

'Get the winch over.'

There was a winch fixed to the deck. It had an arm that could swivel around and was generally used for loading. We swung it about and got some ropes and nets connected under the shark and then used the winch to hoist it up. Then we moved the winch, released the ropes, and dropped the carcass over the side.

'Look –'

Martin was at the rail, face down, head poked over, watching it fall. It hadn't gone far before all the local predators were after it, chasing it down through the sky, hoping to get a couple of bites in before it fell into the sun.

'Oh wow . . . And that could have been us.'

'And look at this. Just great. Just what we need.'

Peggy was standing looking down at the solar panels, every one of them broken.

'Any of them working, Gran?' I said.

'I don't think so. Some might be repairable – if we had the parts. But I don't carry that many spares. The rest, they'll need replacing.'

Martin looked at the wreckage.

'Oh dear,' he said.

'Yes, Martin,' Peggy said. 'Oh dear.' And that was about as near to reproaching him as she got. 'Oh dear, indeed.'

'Sorry,' Martin said. 'About the leftovers. I never thought . . . I didn't realise for a moment that they'd attract –'

'Well, we know now.'

'So what are we going to do, Peggy?'

'Head for land, I guess. Not much choice. Try and make some repairs.'

'We've still got the wind sails.'

Peggy wet a finger and held it up.

'Got the wind sails, but don't have the air to fill them, do we? Wind sails alone won't get us there, Gemma. Not this side of half-term. Limp in on wind sails, and by the time we get to City Island another set of holidays will have begun.'

'Sorry, Gran . . .'

'It's all right, Martin. You weren't to know. But you know now, right? You've learned something. OK?'

'I suppose so,' he said, but he said it reluctantly.

'OK. Let's get this mess cleared up and then we'll get started.'

'Where'll we head for?'

'I'll look at the charts. The nearest friendly island.'

I got a broom and Martin got a pan and a brush and we scraped the bits of sky-shark off the deck and tidied up the shattered solar panels.

'There's an island about eight hours' sailing away,' Peggy said. 'According to these charts. Might take us longer if we're just using wind sails. And it's out of our way. But never mind. Can't be helped.'

Peggy changed the charts around and propped the new one up by the wheel. She altered course and adjusted the sails and we set off from our bearings at about ninety degrees to port.

'Sorry, Peggy.'

'All right, Martin. Don't keep apologising. Too much apologising makes things worse, not better.'

'Anyone want a cup of green tea?'

Which made her smile.

'OK, Martin. Yes. Thank you.'

He went down to the galley. Botcher followed him. Whenever anyone went down to the galley, Botcher always went there too. He didn't necessarily get anything, but he must have felt it was worth a try.

Ten minutes later Martin was back with three bowls of green tea and a bowl of water for you-know-who.

'Thank you, Martin.'

'So what's the name of the island, Peggy?' I asked.

She was reluctant to tell me.

'I can't really read what it says on the chart,' she said. 'Old eyes. I need a test and new glasses. Not had one in more than ten years. I'll get them done at City Island.'

'Want me to look?'

'No, it's OK. I mean, I can make out what it says. I just think it's a mistake or something.'

'Why? What's it say?'

'Well . . . it says here . . .' She pointed at the shape of

a small island on the sky chart. 'Says here that it's called Ignorance.'

'Ignorance?'

'Ignorance. But that can't be right. Maybe a misprint or a misspelling. I think what they really meant is Innocence.'

'Innocence. Yes. That's a nice name for an island,' I said, getting warmed to the place already. 'Innocence – kind of sunshine and a few trees bending in the breeze, and a natural rock spring with sweet water.'

'That's it.' Peggy smiled. 'That's the one. And that's where we're heading. We'll get the solar engines fixed in no time.'

'Be a weird place if it really is called Ignorance,' Martin chimed in, peering over Peggy's arm to see the map.

'It's a mistake,' Peggy said. 'They copied it down wrong.'

'I mean, who'd call an island Ignorance? Calling a place Ignorance, that's just well . . . downright ignorant, if you ask me.'

'It's a mistake, Martin. There's nowhere called Ignorance, believe me. No one is going to call an island Ignorance.'

So we drank our green tea and let the slow hours pass as the soft, poor breezes carried us interminably along through the sky. The wind was just a ripple really, not properly blowing at all, more just breathing gently, like someone asleep.

We dozed, we played I Spy – but that sure is hard in the middle of nowhere when there is nothing much to see, and so Martin started cheating and being stupid and I got fed up with the game.

Then, at last, we saw a distant island to which we drew

ever nearer, until eventually we could make out signs of habitation; there were clusters of ornate buildings and fine houses on one side of it, but on the other there was a kind of shanty town of makeshift, temporary-looking structures and banged-together homes. These were patchwork and multicoloured and crowded in close together. It was a *barrio*, a ghetto, a township – so Peggy said – the kind of place where poor immigrants might live as they waited for opportunity to come their way and to get a handhold on a better life.

'There's the harbour!' Martin called. He was at the prow, holding Peggy's old telescope up to his eye. 'And there's the name sign.'

And there it was too. Proud and tall, standing up on the hills, visible for a long way.

IGNORANCE, it read. NO FINER PLACE TO BE.

'Peggy,' I said. 'It is called Ignorance. It looks like the chart was right after all.'

'Yes,' she said, with a sour note to her voice. 'Doesn't it though?'

She didn't sound at all happy about it.

'Take the sails in, will you, Gemma?'

I went and lowered them, and we drifted in to land. Some people were gathered on the jetty; they were short and squat, but friendly-looking, dressed in tattered clothes. Some didn't even have sandals, just a pair of shorts and a T-shirt.

We threw them a line and they helped us tie up.

'Thank you!' I called.

But as I did, a slim, elegant and finely dressed woman

71

appeared. She was a head or more taller than the labourers on the jetty and was beautifully manicured and had high-lighted hair. Her arms and fingers and ankles and throat were laden with bracelets and jewellery.

'It's all right. There's no need to thank them. They're only Drools. But do step onto our island. You're very welcome. It's not often we get visitors.' And she took us in with her eyes, and weighed us up in her estimation. 'Of any description,' she added. 'Guests are quite a novelty here. So please, do join us.'

She indicated the jetty. So we followed the sweep of her hand and got down from the boat and joined her.

'And are you all the people on board?' she said, as if she expected us to have a few servants along to carry the bags and stir the tea.

'We are. I'm Peggy,' Gran said. 'And these are . . . well . . . these are kin. Great-great-grand-niece and nephew. Gemma and Martin. We need to make some repairs to our solar engines. I was taking them to City Island, but we ran into trouble.'

'Oh, City Island! What fun. I haven't been there in ten turnings or more. Were you going for the shopping? Or the opera?'

'We're going there so they can get an education,' Peggy told the woman, who clapped her hands together at this news, as if it were all great fun and so frightfully amusing.

'Education!' she said. 'How quaint! Oh, wait until I tell the others. They will be entertained. But anyway, do come along. Come on up to the house and let me introduce you.'

72

'Erm, but how about –?'

'No, don't worry about your boat. The Drools will look after it. They'll do all that. You won't need to do anything. They'll fix the solar engines for you. They're ever so clever in their way, at practical things and so on. So good with their hands, you know. Just maybe not so much up top. We leave all the manual work to them.'

'I can fix it myself,' Peggy said. 'I just need the –'

But the woman wouldn't have it.

'Oh, no, no, no,' she said. 'I won't hear of it. No, you can't possibly get your hands dirty. That's a Drool's job. They don't mind it. They enjoy it, really.'

'We're not afraid of getting our hands dirty,' Martin piped up. 'We can get them dirty as you like. Peggy's never been against working and getting your hands dirty. Honest toil, right, Gran?'

The tall woman let another flow of golden, tinkling laughter spill from between her perfect teeth and out of her rosebud mouth.

'Oh, isn't he just so cute,' she said. 'Isn't he such an absolute darling?' And she actually ruffled his hair, which if I'd done it, would have been suicide. But Martin could hardly kick her, so he just glared.

And I thought to myself, is that really my brother Martin you're talking about? Cute? Darling? Martin?

How ignorant can you be, lady? I thought.

But I was about to find that out.

# 7

# the villa

**GEMMA STILL REMEMBERING:**

'We can walk it,' Peggy said, as we left the harbour and saw the houses up on the hill.

'Oh no,' the lady said. 'Really. You can't possibly.'

'It doesn't look far. And we've been cooped up on the boat. It would be nice for us to stretch our –'

'No, really. It's what the Drools are for. They'd be upset if you wouldn't let them transport you. Just take a chair each and they'll carry us up the hill.'

Sedan chairs, Peggy told me later, is what they were called. Two poles, a chair, one Drool at the front, one at the back, up they lift you and away you go.

Our little convoy set out, following the sedan chair carrying Tania, which turned out to be the lady's name. Peggy followed her, then Martin, and I was last.

The two men carrying my chair were like the ones we had seen on the jetty – short, squat, and poorly dressed.

But their eyes were bright and alert, and to me, far from being mere drudges, they appeared keenly intelligent. Calling them Drools seemed nothing better than a deliberate insult. They were friendly and cheerful too, but I had the sense that they were watching and waiting and biding their time. But for what, I didn't know.

They carried us along through the small town and up the hill in the direction of a large villa which surely had to have a fine view of the coast. I could see the back of the man at the front of my chair; the muscles of his neck were knotted; sweat soon began to appear on his skin.

On we went. We passed more tall and elegant people. Tania knew and greeted them all, and called that we were visitors, and everyone and anyone was invited to her villa for drinks.

Her friends regarded us with curious looks and smiles. And every single one of these tall, elegant people had a couple of Drools alongside, carrying the shopping, or waiting to move the people on in their sedan chairs. I noticed as we passed that the Drools were behind the shop counters, that they worked in the restaurants, and that they swept the streets. In fact, it was the Drools who did everything, while the better-off people did nothing. The rich-looking ones were completely idle. But the Drools were all business and industry.

'Who lives there?' I heard Peggy ask, as we went on up the hill. The road narrowed and began to spiral. To our left, at a distance, was another shanty town.

'Oh, the Drools,' Tania answered languidly. 'They have their space. We have ours. But it all works frightfully well. They know how to run everything and we let them get on with it. I couldn't even iron a pillowcase, myself. But then, I don't need to, not with the Drools about. Do you have many Drools on your island?'

'None,' Peggy said, rather curtly too.

'Well, good Lord! Then who does the work?'

'We do,' Peggy said.

'Oh, how marvellous! How awfully original. No Drools? How frightfully old-fashioned. I don't know how we'd manage without our Drools. And doing things for yourself, isn't it just so tiring?'

'It's better than sitting there,' I heard Peggy mutter. 'On your butt all day.' But I don't know if Tania caught what she said, as Peggy followed up her comment with a question. 'What's going on there?'

At the edge of the shanty town a building was going up. It was a good-sized villa, it seemed to me, or it would be when it was completed.

Tania's eyes glanced across to it; her expression registered mild distaste.

'Oh, yes –' Her face (*patrician* and *aristocratic*, I was later to discover, were the words that applied to it) clouded briefly, with perplexity and slight annoyance. But these clouds soon vanished. 'Yes, it's a Drool, apparently. Building himself a villa. Casper, he's called. Top Drool or something. No idea where he gets the money from. Yes. Odd really. They seem to be getting better off, the Drools. Not uppity. We wouldn't have that. Reynold, my husband – whom you'll meet – he'd speak to them if they got uppity. But they do seem to be getting better off.'

76

And then we were at the villa. The Drools set down the sedan chairs they had carried us in and wiped the streaming perspiration from their faces.

'Well, do come in and have some refreshments,' Tania said, leading us into the shade of the villa. 'You must all be so hot and thirsty from that trek up the hill.'

So we followed her into the villa, leaving the Drools out in the bright, hot sunlight.

'Don't they get a drink?' Peggy said.

Tania looked at her, surprised.

'Who?'

'They just carried us up the hill.'

'Oh – the Drools . . . why, yes . . . they'll have some water somewhere. Well, come on in and meet everyone. It's so rare that we have guests.'

We passed some more Drools who were sweeping the floors; others were carrying produce. I glanced into the kitchen and saw Drools at work.

'Reynold . . .' He was even taller and more languid than she was. 'We have visitors. A lady and her two . . . sort of grandchildren. Their boat's being repaired.'

And we were introduced.

'Very pleased to meet you,' Reynold said. 'And welcome to Ignorance.'

'I've got a question,' Peggy said, 'to ask you about that.'

'It's all perfectly simple really,' Reynold said. By now we all had long cool drinks in our hands – a Drool had brought them in – and plates of fresh fruit and snacks. 'Are you at all familiar with the old world poets?'

'Not as familiar as I would like to have been,' Peggy answered, keeping an admirably straight face and not letting a single crinkle of sarcasm crack the veneer. 'And the memory does go a little at my age.'

'It's Shakespeare I'm thinking of,' Reynold went on.

'Never heard of him,' Martin said. 'Was he any good?'

'You'll hear plenty about him at City Island,' Peggy said.

'He did coin one or two memorable phrases,' Reynold continued. 'Ignorance being one of them.'

'Ignorance?'

'"When ignorance is bliss, 'tis folly to be wise." Correct, Tania?'

'Absolutely, darling.'

'That one we're familiar with,' Peggy said.

'And that was the basis of my father's entire philosophy,' Reynold told us.

'That you're better off being ignorant?' Peggy said.

'Exactly.' Reynold smiled. 'Or happier, anyway. If you don't have a clue how to do the unpleasant and laborious things in life, you won't be expected to do them, will you, darling?'

'You will not, dear. More to drink? I'll ring for a Drool.'

More cool drinks appeared. A Drool came and went.

'My father made his money in mining,' Reynold continued. 'In the Uranium Islands. Made billions. Then he sold up. And when he died, he left the money to me, and we bought this island, moved in with some like-minded people, christened the place Ignorance – in a tongue-in-cheek, ironical sort of way – and we've been here ever since: lotus eaters.'

'Lotus –?' I said.

'It means, young lady, that we do nothing but enjoy ourselves, all day long. We neither reap nor sow, nor toil, nor spin. We simply enjoy life, don't we, Tania?'

'To the full.'

'We don't know how to do anything practical and we don't get our hands dirty and we don't do anything we don't want to.'

'We leave all that to the Drools.'

Peggy was looking as sour as the lemon slice in her drink. I knew from old that if there was one thing Peggy did not approve of, it was doing nothing.

'And so where did *they* come from?' she said. 'The workers?'

'The Drools? We brought a few with us. They had their own little island but couldn't make a living there – terribly barren, terribly poor place. And the rest of them just followed later. And they do seem to breed at quite a rate. But they're marvellous little people really. No resentment or envy in them. Do anything for you.'

Peggy looked at Reynold.

'And you're sure about that?' she said.

'I'm sorry?'

'No resentment –?'

'Oh, absolutely none. It's not in their character. Just love looking after you. Born to serve, you see. That's Drools.'

'And what if the money runs out?' Peggy went on. Our

hosts plainly didn't like her questions, which seemed to be making them uncomfortable.

'Well, I don't think that's about to happen any time soon, is it, dear?' Tania said. And Reynold let out a hearty, if somewhat forced and artificial, laugh.

'No. It is rather hard to get through a few billion,' he said. 'No sooner have you spent some than your interest and dividends come in, and you wind up with even more. In fact, what people don't realise about an awful lot of money, is that it just multiplies, all on its own. It's quite impossible to spend it all. So, run out of it – no, I don't think that's about to happen. Ah, that sounds like the door, darling. Our first guests must be arriving. I'll ring for a Drool to bring some drinks.'


The villa began to fill up with more fine and elegant people. Whether they were also wealthy or whether they too lived on Reynold's billions, I didn't know and felt it would be rude to ask.

We were quite the celebrities at that gathering – or quite the novelties anyway. I did wonder if all these rich, elegant people, with no work to do, were not more than a little bored with their lives. But maybe not. There were stylish sky-yachts moored up at the coast, some of them bigger than mansions; perhaps they travelled, went sky-skiing, went deep sky-fishing, or amused themselves in any of a hundred expensive ways.

'I don't like it here.' Martin came over to me. 'Do you like it?'

'No.'

'There's something creepy about the place.'

'I know.'

'What is it?'

'Menace,' I told him. 'Unease.'

'No, it's not that.'

'What then?'

'I don't know. Something in the air. And how can they stand having nothing to do? And not knowing how to do anything, or how anything works. I like knowing how things work. Don't you?'

'Yes, I guess I do.' Though I hadn't really thought of it before.

Peggy got away from a conversation she plainly didn't want to be involved in.

'We'll go soon,' she said.

'What about the boat?'

'They'll have done it by now. It's a couple of hours' work at most.'

But Reynold overheard her.

'Oh, I really don't think so. Your boat won't be ready for days. Smashed solar engine, wasn't it? That'll take a week to fix at the very least.'

'It'll *what*?' Peggy stared at him.

'Oh yes. Had a small meteorite land on our yacht, smashed a solar, got my top Drool on the case, took him a week and cost a small fortune. But don't worry about the cost of yours. You're our guests. Put it on my tab.'

Peggy bristled.

'I pay my way,' she said. 'Always have, always will.

When I get to be a charity case, that's when you can start stitching up the winding sheet.'

'Really, Peggy, it's not a problem. I've told a Drool to get your rooms ready. You can stay with us.'

'Thanks, but I don't think we'll need to. We'll be on our way shortly. I'll just go down and check on progress.'

'Very well. If you insist. If you want to go and look at it, I'll order the sedans.'

'We,' Peggy said, 'will walk.'

Reynold looked at her as if she were mad.

'Walk?'

'Yes, walk. Back down to the harbour.'

'But you can't do that.'

'Why not? It's downhill, isn't it?'

'Only Drools walk.'

'We're walking too.'

'Why?'

'We like walking.'

'But – that's not how we do things here. You don't *need* to walk.'

'I *want* to walk,' Peggy said. 'I want to feel the ground under my feet and stretch my old legs.'

'But –'

'What?'

'The Drools might think . . . that you're Drools too.'

'Let them think it.'

'They might try to strike up a conversation with you.'

'Fine by me. I'll talk to anyone. So'll they. Won't you?'

She turned to us. Martin and I just had to nod.

'Well, really . . . I don't know what to say . . .' Reynold spluttered.

'Thanks for your help and hospitality. We won't break up the party. We'll just slip out. Say goodbye to Tania for us.'

'Your boat won't be ready. When you've checked on the progress, just come back here.'

'It'll be ready.'

So we had to put down our long, cool drinks in the tall, crystal glasses, and slip out into the heat and dust of the day, and we took the track that descended through the dusty town of Ignorance and led us to the harbour.

It was weird. People stared at us, both the ones in the sedan chairs and the Drools. The occupants of the chairs just looked baffled, or slightly offended, at our appearance. They tugged the curtains shut, to keep the insects and the dust and the sight of us out.

The Drools made me uneasy. They weren't like they had been when we were with Tania and being carried around in sedans. They looked sly now, more than clever; cunning, rather than intelligent. They seemed like opportunists, just waiting for a chance to come along. And while before they had appeared kind, now they seemed to have a latent brutality, as if they boiled inside with simmering resentment and a sense of long-harboured injustice.

Once or twice we were jostled and shoved. These incidents could have been accidents, but I didn't feel they were. Martin was the same height as most of the Drools, only he was still growing, whereas they were done with it. They didn't seem to mind him; it was as if he was one of them;

but I was elbowed and pushed, and so was Peggy; there was no respect for age.

We made it to the harbour. Some Drools were gathered by our boat. They looked up at our approach. One of the Drools was better dressed than the others. Not for him old shorts and T-shirts. His clothes were as good as Reynold's had been, though he lacked Reynold's height.

'How is it? Is it done?'

'My dear lady . . . Casper Jones, at your service.'

Peggy gave him the once-over.

'So? Is it done?'

'Done? My dear lady, your solar engines were completely smashed. And not just that. The alternator too, and the solenoids and the heat exchanger and, well . . . a whole host of other matters too technical for you to understand.'

'Try me,' Peggy said.

Casper smiled indulgently and made a gesture with his hands.

'It's complicated, madam. Only a Drool can fix this. A lady like yourself –'

And the other Drools around him nodded in agreement.

'Get out the way,' Peggy said. She got onto the deck and inspected the solar engine. We followed her on board. The solar panels had all been replaced. I couldn't really see what else needed to be done.

'As you can see –' Casper began.

'As I can see,' Peggy said, 'the alternator is fine – and needs a new coil at most, which can be fitted in five minutes. The solenoid has got nothing to do with it and isn't broken anyway. Because there is no solenoid. So I don't know what you're talking about. And as for the heat exchanger, it isn't even up on deck, is it? So how could it have got damaged? Huh?'

Casper's mouth dropped open. The other Drools looked at him expectantly. He cleared his throat.

'Madam – knows – about solar engines?' he began, diffidently now.

'Madam does,' Peggy said. 'Madam installed the engine. Madam built the boat.'

Casper looked the other Drools. They looked back at him.

'Madam – built the boat?' he echoed.

'Madam did,' Peggy said. 'With madam's own two hands. And a bit of help from madam's friends.'

And she stuck her hands out so he could get a look at them and admire the calluses.

'Ah,' Casper said. 'I see –'

Some replacement parts were on the dock side. Peggy started picking through them and holding them up.

'Madam –' Casper wanted to stop her.

'Here we are. New coil. That'll do it. Hand me that screwdriver and the ratchet thing.'

'Madam, this is a Drool's job –'

'And don't get in the way now –'

Casper and the five Drools beside him watched silently as Peggy replaced the alternator coil.

'OK. Martin, go and turn the key and look at the charge meter.'

He disappeared for all of half a minute.

'It's all working,' he said. 'Full reading. Full charge.'

'Right. Here's your tools back. Tell me what I owe you for parts and labour, and I think we're done and on our way.'

Casper never took his eyes off her. There was something in that look, as if he could cheerfully have killed her.

'How much do I owe you? You know?'

'Of course, madam, of course. But Mr Reynold let me know in advance that all works should be charged to his account. It just requires a signature from you.'

'We pay our own way. What's the damage?'

Before Casper could say anything further, she plucked the bill from his hands.

'What?'

Casper looked defiant but uncomfortable.

'I could buy a new boat for this.'

'Madam is maybe not familiar with the price of solar panels –'

'No. Madam is very familiar. And not only that, Madam knows a rip-off when she sees one. And madam is not paying this. Gemma, go and get my purse from the strongbox.'

Down I went, got the purse, then back onto the deck. Peggy took out a note worth a hundred International Currency Units.

'Keep the change,' she said, and handed it to Casper.

'But the bill says –'

'I can see what the bill says, and one thousand twelve hundred Units is a little pricey for new panels costing fifty. The other fifty's for your labour. I regard the additional thousand you have down here for the work as also excessive.

So there's your money. I'll thank you for your time and trouble. Now, if you'll excuse us, we'll be on our way.'

Peggy held the money out for him to take. Reluctantly, he took it.

'Now, you just write *Paid* there on that bill. OK? Then everything'll be settled and we'll be gone.'

I didn't think he would agree to do it, but he felt in his coat pocket for a pen. He clicked it open. He smiled at Peggy humourlessly and without warmth.

'Madam really doesn't understand how things are done here –' he began.

'Yes, I do,' Peggy said. She pointed to the top of the hill. 'They have the money. But you have the knowledge. So you rob them blind. And because they don't know any better, they go on paying. And you're building yourself a brand-new house, there on the corner of the shanty town. And, little by little, you're moving up the hill, Mr Casper. Is that not right?'

Casper smiled more broadly and with a little more warmth, unabashed to have been discovered, pleased to have his cleverness revealed.

'And one day, correct me if I'm wrong, but one day, sooner or later – and probably sooner, I'm guessing, though I don't really know why –'

'Gut instinct, madam?' Casper gave a sardonic, tight-lipped smile.

'Possibly so. But one day soon, something will happen – some incident – some tipping point – and the people with the knowledge on this island are going to take over from

87

the ones who are ignorant. And I wouldn't be surprised if one twilight time – if you get night-time here –'

'We do indeed, madam,' Casper said, and he indicated a satellite island that had come in to orbit between the island of Ignorance and the sun. 'Our satellite isle. We call it Bliss.'

'One twilight time, when the international police patrol ships are nowhere to be seen, it wouldn't surprise me to see a whole crowd of people flocking up that hill, up to those fine villas, carrying torches and firebrands – and then, well . . . topsy-turvy, I think, Mr Casper. Would that be right?'

The smile didn't go; it remained on his face, fixed and friendly.

But, 'I think that might be right, madam,' he said, in all but a whisper. 'Madam is a wise old lady.'

'No. Not wise. Just not ignorant,' Peggy said. 'Thank you for your help, Mr Casper. If it's all right with you, we'll be on our way.'

'Be my guest, madam.'

'Then we'll say goodbye.'

He didn't have to let us go. He could easily have stopped it. There were dozens of Drools milling around the harbour. It wouldn't have taken much to prevent us. But he let us sail. And soon there was safe, unbridgeable space between us. We could easily have catcalled and thumbed our noses. But, for some reason, that felt like the last thing you wanted to do.

As we sailed out into open space, we saw the satellite isle of Bliss come between Ignorance and the sun, and night-time came to them there, and the darkness leaked up around the island, and the villas and the town disappeared from view, swallowed by night.

But then, the strangest thing happened. Lights appeared. Small, flickering lights; a few at first, and then more and more, as if people were lighting matches, only these lights didn't burn out. They appeared to congregate, to gather together and then to move, in a kind of procession, and to rise as they went, as if marching through the main street of the town of Ignorance and going up into the hills.

And then there was the far, far sound of voices calling, but so far away it was like the sound of distant rain falling into a lake. And then the small flames ignited into larger ones, which were taken by the wind, and soon the hills were on fire.

And we watched the flames, and the villas burning, and we didn't say a word to each other, not one single word, until I couldn't bear the silence any longer and I had to speak the thoughts that were going through my mind.

'So ignorance is bliss, is it –?'

'And knowledge is power, Gemma,' Peggy said. 'Knowledge is power.'

She came and stood between us, and put her arms around us both. And we stood and watched the houses burning, and we heard the distant shouts and cries for help, though there was nothing we could do to help anyone. And then she gently, very gently, turned our heads away.

# 8

# martin again

**MARTIN SPEAKING AGAIN (GEMMA GETS A REST):**

Sometimes, back on Peggy's island, I'd find something lying around – like a metal rod or an old stick or something – and I'd pretend it was a gun, and go shooting things up. Peggy saw me doing so once, and said, 'Martin, where did you get *that* from?'

'Picked it up, Peggy,' I said. 'It was lying on the shore.'

You get all kinds of stuff drifting in on the solar tide. I found some money once, paper notes. I gave them to Peggy and she locked them away for the future.

Of course, it's only light and feathery stuff that drifts in. Anything substantial, it starts to sink in the atmosphere, picking up speed as it goes, and then it's that big, dry splash and a moment's flickering as it burns up in the sun.

'I don't mean where did you get the piece of wood from. I mean, where did you get the idea to turn it into a gun and go bang-banging around the place?'

Well, I didn't know. The idea just sort of came to me. I didn't make any effort to think it up.

'I don't know, Peggy. It was kind of . . . inspiration.'

At which she gave me one of her one-hundred-and-twenty-year-old hard-pickled looks.

'Inspiration? Not what I'd be calling it. More the sort of thing a hooligan might do.'

'What's a hooligan, Peggy?'

'Someone who likes a fight and causing trouble. You'll be able to look it up in the big dictionary when we go to City Island.'

'Won't it be in the little dictionary?' I said.

'It will,' Peggy agreed. 'But small dictionaries just give small definitions. Besides, my dictionary's ninety years old if it's a turning. And words can change their meanings.'

Which surprised me somewhat.

'Words can change their meanings?'

'Sometimes, Martin.'

'How?'

'They just do.'

'But isn't that kind of like . . . changing your name? Like, a Martin is a Martin. How could "Martin" change its meaning? That would make me someone else.'

'It's called common usage. You take a word like *wicked*. Once, wicked meant bad and evil. Then it came to mean pretty good and excellent stuff. But as far as I know, a hooligan is still a hooligan. But, as I'm ninety years out of touch, maybe a hooligan is someone saintly by now.

But anyway, put the gun down, Martin, and don't stick it in my face.'

'I was only playing . . .'

'Yeah. I know. What's bothering me is why.'

'I don't know. I was just pretending.'

'I just don't know what put the idea into your head. You don't see Gemma bang-banging at things.'

'She's not so perfect.'

'That's not what I'm saying. Perfection doesn't come into it. It's the ways we're imperfect is the trouble. Some imperfections are more tolerable than others.'

I'd seen Gemma pulling the fins off sky-fish when we were smaller. I don't say she did it out of evil, more out of curiosity, and I'd never seen her do it since. But no one's perfect is all I'm getting at and there are other ways to be a hooligan than to go bang-banging with a pretend gun. It's just that sisters are more hooligans on the quiet and the sly. Girls do nasty things too, seems to me, but they're more likely to get away with it, as they try and look angelic afterwards so nobody would suspect.

'I think I got the idea from old Ben Harley,' I said. 'He's got a gun.'

'Yes, you're right,' Peggy said. 'He has, hasn't he? He's got that old harpooner. And if he goes on drinking that private stash of his the way he does, he's going to end up shooting himself in the foot.'

'Would that hurt?' I asked, wondering if we might hear Ben Harley yelling when he finally got round to shooting himself in the foot, even though his island was quite some distance away.

'What do you think, Martin?'

'It would hurt.'

'It would hurt like hell. He'll end up walking round on a wooden leg, if he's not careful. Though no doubt it would match his wooden brain.'

'Thought we weren't supposed to use words like hell, Peggy.'

'No, kiddo. You're not to use words like hell. I get to use them whenever I like.'

'Why's that, Peggy? Isn't that like don't do as I do but do as I –?'

'No it isn't. It's not do as I say at all. I don't want you saying as I say, or you'll end up a foul-mouthed hick from the way-backs, and when you get to City Island they'll think you're a little savage – which, going by that gun there, they may have some grounds for supposing.'

'So why's it all right for you to say words like hell, Peg, and not me?'

'Because I'm one hundred and twenty years old and I've paid my dues and you're not and you haven't.'

'So when I'm a hundred and twenty years old and I've paid my dues can I say words like hell then?'

'You seem to be saying them now, far as I can hear.'

'I mean, can I go saying them on a regular basis?'

'Martin, if you ever get to be my age, you can swear like a trooper all day long. You have my permission.'

'Will you give me a note saying I can do that?'

'The hell I will.'

'You're saying it again, Peggy.'

'I've got provocation.'

'What?'

'You. You and that damn toy gun.'

'You've gone and said damn now, Peggy.'

'The hell I have.'

'No, you did. I heard you say it.'

'Martin, find something else to play with, can't you? I don't like guns.'

'But you've got a harpooner too. Hidden away. I've seen it.'

'Really? Well, two things about that. One, what are you doing rummaging about in my hidden-aways?'

'I came upon it by accident.'

'The hell you did. Two, that harpooner is for emergencies only, big emergencies. I don't like guns, Martin. Not even pretend ones. You play at war and soldiers and shooting things, next thing you know you're all grown up and you are a soldier and you *are* shooting things. Only, after you've pulled the trigger, what you pointed the gun at doesn't get up.'

'Oh, I was only passing the time, Peg.'

'I know. I know you're a good person at heart, Martin. It's just sometimes playing at something is conditioning, preparation, you might say, for the real thing.'

'Well, I'll throw it away then.'

'No, you don't have to do that. I'm not forbidding it. You play with it as much as you like.'

'I don't really want to any more.'

'Well, you want to come and help me go rock-combing?'

'Yes, OK. Think we'll find anything today?'

'You never know.'

So I just left the piece of wood by the coast there and we went rock-combing – which is searching the rocks for whatever the wind and solar tide might have brought in. Most of it's rubbish, but you occasionally find useful stuff.

Anyhow, what put me in mind of all this, after we left the island of Ignorance and continued on our way with our repaired and working solar engines back intact, was what appeared in the sky a day or two later. It happened on my watch, too, which is why I so exactly remember all the details and such.

It's mostly boring being on watch. Boring but – according to Peggy – necessary. The Toll Troll had proved that. (You know, I think I maybe use that expression a lot, or even too much. *According to Peggy*. Most of what I know is *according to Peggy*. I think maybe she ought to write her memoirs and put down all her choice phrases and sayings and call it *According to Peggy*.

But I don't know if anyone would publish it as it would be full of hells and damns, and a whole lot worse, and the righteous (whom Peggy doesn't have much time for) would say it was disgusting and try to have it banned, which would probably tickle her pink no end, and maybe even tickle her yellow too. Because, why does it have to be pink that you're tickled? I don't know. I don't see why you can't be a whole rainbow tickled – even tickled infrared and ultraviolet, come to that.

Occasionally, in among the tedium, being on watch has its interesting moments too. Because you never know what might come along: a sky-whaler chasing a sky-whale, sky-jellies, an algae bloom, a full-on midge swarm – and they have to be seen to be believed.

They travel through the sky like tornadoes. If you can't avoid a midge bloom, they'll cause you misery untold. They get into everything: your eyes, lungs, throat, down in your clothes, into the galley, the food, every crevice of the ship. Even Ben Harley's private stash won't repel a whole swarm of midges. It's said that if you get enough of them, they can strip a sky-shark to the bone. One minute it's a sky-shark, the next it's just a skeleton flying through the air. Don't know if I believe that, but it's what Ben Harley says.

So it was my watch and I had the scope to my eye and I was looking. I looked here, I looked there. I didn't see anything except blue sky and a few tiny clouds and some black spots that had to be islands in the far, far away. That or dirt on the lens.

I took a rest. Peggy and Gemma were sprawled on the deck, both with their eyeshades on and both asleep and snoring. I mean, when I'd been asleep they'd say to me, 'Martin, you were snoring again.' Or, 'Martin, you were talking in your sleep.' Or, 'Martin, would you like to know what you were doing when you were dozing back then?'

And they'd make out that when it came to them they

were all ladylike and dainty sleepers. But the truth was, they were driving them home like saw-fish. But whenever I told them that they both snored something terrible, they wouldn't believe me, and made out it was sour grapes and I was making it all up. So that's girls for you as far as I could tell – big snorers but pretending otherwise. Not that Peggy's a girl, but she was once.

When I tackled her on the subject of girls and snoring, she said it would be different when we got to City Island and I would meet girls there I would feel differently about. She said sisters were one thing but other girls were another. So I was reserving my judgement on that score and was waiting to see what these other girls might be like, and as far as I was concerned, they were innocent until proven guilty. But if they were going to tell me they never snored, I wouldn't believe them. As I'd already had experience.

Well, I took a drink of water and I put the telescope back to my eye. There were a few sky-fish around and some small sky-jellies, but they were the harmless ones that weren't going to bother you. I raised the scope a little and looked above us. There, in the distance, I could make something out. It was still small, but it was moving, and it was coming our way. I kept the scope trained on it and tightened the focus a little. Then I prodded Gemma with my foot and I shook Peggy by the arm.

'Something coming,' I said. 'Something funny-looking.'

And it *was* funny-looking too. It was weird. The shape of it was wrong. It couldn't be a sky-fish. I knew what they looked like. I knew every kind and variety that lived up at our level, and even the names of some of the leathery ones from down below that we had hauled up sometimes on great long lines.

Gemma stretched and stood up and Peggy did the same, but she took a little longer and she creaked more.

'Let me see, Martin –' Peggy said.

I handed her the scope.

'It looks a bit like a sky-fin, but if it is, there's something else with it . . .'

Peggy held the scope to her eye and then passed the scope to Gemma.

'What do you think?'

'It's a rider.'

Gemma handed the scope back to me.

'It's a what?' I said.

I looked again. I'd never seen anything like this. She was right – there was a rider on the back of the sky-fin. The sky-fin was saddled and bridled and somehow broken in and tamed, and the rider was using it as private transport, and the mount was speeding him through the sky.

'I knew they were friendly but I thought they were wild. I didn't know you could tame them.'

'If you're got the patience – and the determination – and don't mind getting a few bites and tail slaps along the way,' Peggy said. 'Or you can whisper them, if you have the gift.'

'Whisper them?'

'Persuade them and cajole them – with sweet nothings in their ears. You don't need whips and spurs when you've got sweet nothings and you know how to say them. Just brings them round and calms them down. But you have to have the knack. Cloud Hunters do it.'

'That a Cloud Hunter?'

'If it is, it's a lost and lonely one. They don't usually travel alone.'

The sky-fin and its rider were heading across our path at fifty degrees. But then abruptly the rider seemed to see us, for he jerked at the bridle and turned the sky-fin around, and he began to head in our direction.

'Looks like he wants some company,' Peggy said. She took the telescope back. 'I wonder . . .' She put the lens to her eye, seemed to stiffen, then, 'Gemma,' she said. 'Go down to the cabin, get my knife and bring it to me.'

Gemma didn't question her and nor did I, and I made out like I wasn't worried neither, but I was. What had Peggy seen about the rider that she wanted her knife for?

'Can't we just change course?' Gemma said. She was back with the knife and the sheath it came in. Peggy hooked it to her belt.

'Wouldn't be any good,' Peggy said. 'A sky-fin, even with extra weight on its back, is going to outrun you easy. Let's just see what he wants. Might all be fine. Why look for trouble?'

She put the telescope down. As Gemma didn't pick it up again, I did. I could see them both clearly now, the sky-fin and the rider. He didn't look much older than Gemma to me, but he looked kind of strange, kind of blank, like there wasn't much going on in his mind – or if there was, he was determined to keep it all to himself.

He wore a bandana around his head to keep his long hair in place and out of his eyes, and both were streaming behind him as the sky-fin rode the thermals and kept on coming, its fins beating so fast they were blurs in the heat haze. I could see already that he had scars on his face – deep, ritual, Cloud Hunters' scars, running from just under his eyes to the corners of his mouth. His torso was bare and he wore camouflage fatigues on his legs. But criss-crossing his bare chest were bandoliers, make out of sky-shark leather, and they held at least a score of short arrows, made from sharpened bone; and slung around his back was a bow, a crossbow.

As he approached, he let go of the reins and dug his knees and ankles into the side of the sky-fin, to keep it on course. Then he reached behind him, brought the crossbow around and loaded it with an arrow. He put a second arrow in a groove on the bow, so that when he fired the first, he could reload almost instantly.

By now I didn't need the telescope any more. I could hear the beating of the sky-fin and the sound of it coming and of the displaced air. Then we could hear its breath and its panting lungs, as it headed straight for us. The rider dug in with his knees and the sky-fin swooped under the hull and reappeared on the port side of our boat. It came to a stop almost immediately, and then there it was, the sky-fin and the rider, hovering just above the deck.

The rider looked at us and now that we could see him close to I realised that he was wasn't a whole lot older than Gemma at all – in fact he wasn't all that much older than me.

He levelled the crossbow and pointed it in Peggy's direction.

'Who's the skipper?'

'You're looking at her, young fella.'

But he disregarded the young fella stuff.

'You're in territorial sky.'

'The hell we are,' Peggy said, at the hells yet again. 'We're in open sky.'

'You're in sky belonging to the Liberation Enlightenment Army.'

'We're damn well not. You look at this chart –'

She reached for the maps, but the rider moved the crossbow so that it pointed straight at her.

'It doesn't matter what the charts say. They're old. This is territorial sky belonging to the Liberation Enlightenment Army and you've no business being here.'

'We've every business –'

'I'm the one talking, old woman –'

Peggy gave him a look but didn't say anything, though it was plain she didn't think much of his manners.

'Turn the boat around, and go where I say.'

'The hell I will.'

He levelled the crossbow.

'You want me to use this? You think I won't?'

Peggy looked at him, and so did I. I looked right into his eyes. I thought he would use the crossbow. I thought he probably already had.

'OK,' Peggy said. 'But it's all a big misunderstanding. Where to?'

'There. Straight ahead. I'll be riding right behind you. I'll give you more directions. Any change of course and –'

To make his point he fired off the arrow in the crossbow; it thwacked into the mast and reverberated, like a violin playing, then it stopped. He'd already reloaded.

'All right?'

'We can hear you,' Peggy said. 'Only where are we heading and what are we going there for?'

'We're going to join the rest of the troops,' the boy said – and he was a boy really, even to call him a young man would be stretching it. 'And find out who you're spying for.'

'Spying?'

'You've got a scope.'

'Every boat's got a scope. Who'd leave land without one?'

'Then maybe you're colluding with the enemy.'

'What enemy? We don't know anything about your wars and squabbles, kid. We don't know who you're fighting nor why you're fighting them. We're just on our way to City Isl—'

'Don't call me kid,' the kid said. 'You hear me?'

'OK,' Peggy said. 'Take it easy – I'm turning her around.'

She took the wheel and turned the boat around steadily.

'OK. Angle up ten degrees and set the auto for thirty degrees to starboard,' he instructed.

'Anything you say.'

'OK. Put the solars on full. Leave the sails as they are.'

'You're the boss.'

'Just do it.'

He jerked the crossbow again, in a kind of general, all-encompassing warning. Or maybe it was more of a threat.

'And no talking.'

So we sailed on in silence, on the course he had given, and he rode behind us on the sky-fin, a few metres back, keeping the crossbow primed and ready, and pointed at Peggy's neck.

I saw, from the corner of my eye, that Gemma was turning her head around slowly to sneak a look at him. But he was onto it immediately and he barked at her to keep her looks straight ahead. But she took her time to turn her head away, and I sensed that he was looking at her too, and that he maybe found her a whole lot more interesting than Peggy, or me, or the sky-fin that was dutifully carrying him along.

And I realised, that apart from me, he was the first real boy Gemma had seen since we had been orphaned and gone to live with Peggy, a whole long eight turnings ago. We'd only known each other. The three of us and old Ben Harley and that's all it was. It was kind of strange to realise that there were other people in the world near your age. And maybe other worlds too. Ones that you could never even dream of.

# 9

# war zone

**MARTIN SPEAKING STILL:**

'You want some water?' Peggy called to him. She poured out a cupful, left it balanced on the rail, and he swooped down on the fin, took the water, drank it and left the empty cup where he had found it. He nodded, but he didn't thank her, and he kept the crossbow pointed at her. The sky-fin didn't get any water. They never drink. They seem to survive on vapour.

We sailed on. The sky was as empty as a pocket. (One of Peggy's sayings, but then she never did have much money.) After half an hour's travelling we saw a cluster of islands, mostly small, some little bigger than rocks.

'There,' he said. 'Cut the solar.'

Peggy closed the shields and we slowed, then drifted.

'We'll see what the troops say.'

But it was hard to see them. I sneaked a look through the telescope, but I couldn't see anyone. Maybe I was looking at the wrong island, so I moved the telescope around, but they all appeared to be deserted, except that on the largest of them there were dark, crouching shapes – many of them, and menacing-looking, as if they were predators, waiting to pounce.

'Tie up.'

We were at a jetty. A bleached, tattered flag fluttered from a post. There was a red fist upon it, against a green background, and the words Liberation Enlightenment Army – Fighting For Freedom.

But when Peggy saw it, she just snorted, and said, 'Aren't they all?' She meant, I guess, that everyone says they're fighting for freedom, even the ones who aren't.

'We'll talk to the comrades.'

He hopped down from the sky-fin and tethered it to a post so it wouldn't fly away. Sky-fins are friendly, but they aren't so friendly that they'll give up their liberty for you. A chance to escape and they're off.

The boy soldier's feet clattered on the planks of the jetty. I saw then that he wasn't wearing sandals, but military boots, which looked several sizes too big for him, and I wondered if he might have plundered them off a corpse.

'This way. You first.'

He waved with the crossbow and along we went.

'Stop right there.'

'There' was just down from the jetty, on a promontory. It was like it had been when we stopped to pay off the Toll Troll, only worse. Because it wasn't just three cairns there – three memorial heaps of stones and pebbles – this was worse, there were scores, maybe a hundred or more.

105

'We've got to ask everyone what to do,' he said. 'We'll ask my friends.'

And he stopped and sat down on a rock, and he waved at us with the crossbow to stand where we were.

I didn't understand, but I hoped that someone did. I looked at Gemma. Her face was pale and sad and she was staring at the boy with the crossbow as if she felt the greatest sympathy for him, pitied him, despite all his swagger and bravado. Then I looked at Peggy, and her eyes were moving from him to the cairns and back.

'Oh my,' she said. 'Oh my.' And she sat down suddenly, on a stone next to the soldier – who didn't look old enough to be any kind of soldier at all. 'Oh my,' she said again. And the boy just looked at her, and he seemed to have forgotten all about the crossbow and the arrows, and his eyes were filling with tears.

'They're all dead,' he said. 'All of them. Everyone.'

And I noticed then that the wind had picked up and that a cool breeze was blowing, ruffling the tattered flag on the post on the jetty. You could hear the cloth slapping against the wire that held it, but other than that, there was barely a sound.

'What's your name?' Peggy asked.

'Alain,' he said. 'Alain Qualar. Colonel. Number 5762.'

'Oh my,' Peggy said again, 'Oh my. I expected to have seen it all by now. But no. Oh my.'

'They're all gone,' he said. 'I'm all that's left. Children's Division, Liberation Enlightenment Army.' And then he seemed to stiffen, as if with some remnant of military pride, and added, 'At your service.'

But while this was going on – and it may not sound very good, but it's the truth all the same – and while Peggy was staring at that boy as if she was looking at the consequences of the worst the world could do to people, and while Gemma was also staring at him, like she wanted to give him some big consoling hug, like he was the most interesting thing she'd ever seen since that dead sky-squid landed in the back garden, all I could think was: I wonder, if I asked him nicely, if he'd give me a go on his crossbow. Because it seemed pretty cool really, and I wouldn't have minded trying it out.

'Alain,' Peggy said. 'Tell me what happened.'

He looked at her, indecisive, unsure as to whether he should – as a military man – allow this kind of familiarity between soldier and prisoners of war; which, in his eyes, was what we were. But his resolve crumbled and it was as if a barrier broke, and all it had held back came tumbling out.

'We were Cloud Hunters,' he said. 'My family. I'd just been initiated –' His hand went up to the scars on his face. 'We'd had a Witnessing. You know about that?'

'We know.' Peggy nodded.

'It was a turning – two turnings – I don't know. I remember the day clearly . . . well, you would. But we were travelling and we met another cloud-hunting boat and my father waved and called them over and asked them to Witness, and they said they would, that it would be an

107

honour – well, that's what they have to say, don't they. That's what you do.'

'You didn't have the scars then?'

'No. I wasn't old enough. I mean, you'd remember your coming of age. But there was something else – on the boat we hailed, there were four Cloud Hunters, two brothers, the wife of one of them, and their daughter. But there was also a boy who was an Islander. No scars, nothing. And they'd taken him along with them for the journey. Which you never see. Cloud Hunters stick together. And I can remember him staring, as my father thrust his knife into the fire, and then brought the red-hot tip up to my face, and cut the scars.'

'Didn't it hurt?' I couldn't help asking.

'Shhh!'

'Martin!'

But Alain didn't mind the question.

'No,' he said. 'Not really. Not then. Afterwards, maybe. You get a potion to drink and it numbs the nerves.'

'Then I wouldn't mind getting some scars too,' I said. But Peggy scowled and Gemma snapped at me again.

'Go on,' I said. 'Sorry to interrupt.'

'After the ceremony we went our different ways. We headed in the direction of the Forbidden Isles, as our tracker said the clouds would be good there, and the other boat sailed towards the island the boy with them called home.'

He was silent a while. I wanted to prompt him, but Peggy stared me quiet.

'Anyway . . . we'd been sailing a few days and the scars on my face were beginning to heal. We could see clouds forming in the far distance and kept on a course to meet them. But then we saw we had company. There were six boats moving across the sky towards us at tremendous speed. They had everything on board – solar engines, wind sails and, along the sides, galley-men with paddles, all pawing at the air in unison to drive the boats along.

'"Barbaroons!" That was what my father thought, and wanted to turn our boat around and try to outrun them, but, as our tracker said, it would have been pointless. Compared to their boats, ours was a snail.

'Yet, as they got nearer, it was plain that they weren't Barbaroons at all. They were too smart, too disciplined, as Barbaroons are usually a scraggy and uncoordinated bunch given to fighting among themselves. No, they were soldiers. But no ordinary ones. They were child soldiers, every one of them. The tallest – their commander – was still in his teens, and he was the eldest. There wasn't an adult among them.

'"Heave to, or we'll blast you out of the air!"

'It wasn't friendly, but it was perfectly clear. So we reeled in the sails and drifted, waiting to see what they might want.

'The eldest of them, in the leading ship, threw a grappling iron out to haul in our boat.

'"What can we do for you?" my father said, keeping it cool and polite. "Gentlemen," he added. "And ladies too," he said, when he saw – as I did – that at least half the child army was composed of girls.

'"We're at war and looking for recruits," their commander said.

'"Who's at war?"

'"The Liberation Enlightenment Army."

'"Not heard of it."

'"You have now."

'"At war with who?"

'"The Oppressionists."

'"Not heard of them either."

'"Then that's something else you've learned today."

'"Well, your war isn't our war," my father said. "Whatever it may be."

'"It is now," the commander said. "It just became your war. That's how wars are, my friend. You have to take a side."

'"We're Cloud Hunters," my father told him. "Cloud Hunters don't get involved in –'

'"We'll take the boy," the Commander said. And then he looked at my sister, who was still only small then. "The girl's too young. You can keep her."

'Well, it's pointless to go into the details, but you can imagine how it was, my father's anger, my mother's grief, my sister crying, our tracker reaching for his knife and nearly getting himself killed. But there was nothing to be done. I had to go or they'd have murdered us all. So I sailed one way, and my family were left behind me, and so – like it or not, willingly or not – I became a member of the Liberation Enlightenment Army.'

'Wow!' I said. 'Amazing. And did you get a uniform and

110

a gun and stuff and learn how to kill people with your bare hands?'

I got the looks again, the Peggy looks and the Gemma looks. But the look I got from Alain was nothing like theirs. Their looks were angry and disgusted. His look was sympathetic and understanding, but kind of sad.

'What's your name, kid?' he said.

'Martin –'

'You'd like to be a soldier, would you, Martin?'

'Yeah,' I said. 'It sounds like – an adventure. I mean, tell me – did you ever shoot anyone?'

He didn't answer immediately. In fact, I didn't think I was going to get an answer at all. But I did, if an oblique one.

'This island that we're on now was the barracks,' Alain continued. 'Barracks and training ground. Where they break your spirit and build it up again. And when you wake from what seems like one long nightmare, you find you've turned into a soldier.'

'Wow . . .' I couldn't help saying that one. It just slipped out. I wasn't trying to be annoying.

'The Liberation Enlightenment Army was one of two factions on one of the Forbidden Isles. They were revolutionaries; their opponents were the junta in power. They explained the politics of it to me, but I could never understand them. All I knew was that we were in the right and the others were in the wrong, and we had God on our side, but they didn't –'

'And they, of course, believed exactly the same, no doubt,' Peggy said. Alain looked at her.

'I don't know,' he said. 'I never really thought of it like that.'

'Why didn't you try to run away and escape?' That was Gemma. Alain swivelled his eyes around to look at her. She looked away before their eyes could make contact.

'They take you up into the hills,' he said. 'Where they keep the prisoners they've taken. And they put a crossbow into your hands. And they say, "You're one of us now. We're your family and we're your friends. You don't have any other family any more. Just us. We're all you have. And we're going to look after you and all we ask in return is your loyalty. And all we ask is that you demonstrate that loyalty to us. So all you have to do is to point the crossbow now, and to pull the trigger."'

I felt suddenly sick. I didn't want to be a soldier any more. I'd thought it was just kind of fun and adventures.

'And if you don't pull the trigger – if you say you don't want to pull the trigger – can't pull the trigger – then they turn their crossbows onto you . . . and . . . well . . . that's the choice,' Alain said. 'Does that answer your question?'

Peggy was staring at him once more, and she looked as old as the universe, as old as time itself, and she just shook her head and she looked so sad, as if she were looking at some terrible disease that there should have been a cure for by now, but there wasn't.

'And that's the choice . . .' Alain said again. 'That's the only choice you have.'

And it didn't look like there was anything anyone could say. There were no patches, no repairs. It was like there was so big a hole in the world that you could never darn it up.

'What happened here, Alain?' Peggy said.

'It's Colonel!' he snapped, like the soldier had come back into him, and he was all steel and bayonets and pack drills and marches, and civilians like us were foreigners from another land. 'Colonel by default. The surviving soldier assumes the higher rank!'

'Sorry . . .' Peggy said. '. . . Colonel.'

He stared back at her, a glint of some kind of madness in his eyes. But then that spark extinguished, and he was just a boy again, a couple of years older than me, with Cloud Hunters' scars on his face.

'No . . . that's all right . . . Alain's fine . . . it's fine.'

I looked at the piles of stones. I couldn't count all the cairns. Peggy said my maths was terrible, despite her best efforts, but it would all be fixed when we got to City Island. I wondered if it would. I wondered if teaching could really fix as much as she claimed, or if there were things in the world that nothing could fix, not education or love or anything. I was starting to suspect there might be damage that could never be repaired.

'I was sent out as a scout – on the sky-fin there. I was gone half a day. When I came back I could see the clouds – too dark for vapour – and the glow of fires. I knew there had been a battle, but I didn't ever imagine . . . You see, most of them, they were all like me, they'd been press-ganged, abducted. It wasn't our war, we were just made to fight it. But when I came back . . . there was no one left alive. I had to do all the rites, all myself – each one sent to the sun – and I made a cairn for them, so that they'd be remembered . . . if anyone came . . . their parents maybe, finally finding them . . . so they'd know . . .'

'And then?' Peggy said. 'How long ago was that?'

'A while,' Alain said. 'I didn't know what else to do . . . I didn't know how to find my family . . . so I went on being a soldier.'

'I think you'd better come with us,' Peggy said.

He flared up with anger again.

'I'm the commander here. I give the orders.'

'It's an invitation, Colonel. Not an order.'

He looked crestfallen, strangely confused.

'I don't know . . .'

'We're going to City Island,' I piped up. 'To get clever. Why don't you come too? And maybe I could get a go on your crossbow –'

'Martin!'

'And Gemma wants you to come with us as well. I'm sure she does. You can see it from her face –'

'Martin! Shut up!'

But it was true. She did want him to come. And she wouldn't have blushed otherwise. So I knew I was right.

Alain stood and walked away, turning his back to us. He left the crossbow. If we'd been quick, one of us could have grabbed it and shot him. Not that we would have, of course. I was probably the only one who thought of that. He kicked at the dust with his military boots. Then he turned to face us.

'I don't think so. I'm a Cloud Hunter. Cloud Hunters wouldn't be wanted on City Island, or any other island.'

'Young man,' Peggy said, at her sternest. 'Right now the government is desperate for educated and intelligent people. It's handing out free educations to whoever wants one. If you've got the brains – and I don't doubt you have them – who cares about the scars on your face? It's what inside your head that matters. And you can't stay here, can you?'

He moved away and walked to where the memorial cairns were. He picked up some loose stones and patted them into place. Those cairns would stand there for thousands of turnings. It would be a long, long time before the sparse rain eroded them and the wind and time crumbled them to dust.

'You might even find your family again – one day. An educated person would know how to look, where to look. You can do anything with an –'

'What about my sky-fin?'

'Set it free. Or take him with you.'

'It's a she.'

'Her with you then.'

'Can I bring her with me?'

'Of course.'

'What are your names?'

'Peggy. Gemma. Martin.'

'I apologise if I –'

'That doesn't matter.'

'I'll just . . . say goodbye.'

'We'll wait for you, at the jetty.'

Which we did. I saw him up by the cairns, saying goodbye to every single one.

'And stop asking him if you can have a go on his crossbow, Martin!'

'I was only asking, Gemma. And what's it got to do with you anyway?'

'You're an embarrassment!'

'I'm the embarrassment? I don't think so. Pity we don't have a mirror on the boat. Then you'd see who the embarrassment is.'

'Hey. You two! That's enough.'

'Well . . .'

Peggy let out one of her sighs. One of those haven't-I-put-up-with-enough? sighs. So we let it drop. But I didn't see why I couldn't have a go on the crossbow at some point.

Alain came to the jetty. All his belongings he carried in a backpack. He untethered the sky-fin and hitched it to the rail of the boat.

'She'll fly along with us,' he said.

Which she did. So we left the island and the cairns behind us, and instead of three of us, there were four now, and we were all headed for City Island, to start studying. And that was going to make all the difference – so one of us said, the old one – and it would change our lives forever and for the better.

But I still wanted a shot at the crossbow.

# 10

# new passenger

**GEMMA SPEAKING AGAIN:**

Well, at least it was nice to finally have somebody young on board who wasn't so constantly and completely juvenile.

I mean, Martin's all right. Up to a point. But there are only so many stupid questions and smarty-pants retorts that you can tolerate. Maybe not all younger brothers are necessarily idiotic, but mine certainly is inclined that way.

The boy didn't talk a lot, not at first. He just sat on the deck, looking out into space – of which there is plenty – and you didn't know if he wanted to be left alone, or if really he wanted you to ask him a question so he could talk about everything that had happened to him.

I told Martin to stop bothering him about the crossbow, but the boy – Alain, that is – said that he didn't mind. He showed Martin how to use it and they drew a target at the far end of the deck and fired at it. Martin was full of himself when he hit the middle of it, so I asked to try, and I hit the bullseye too – Martin was disappointed to see – so it wasn't that difficult.

Peggy just left him alone, probably on her time-heals-all-wounds principle. Maybe she's right about that, or maybe it depends on how much time you've got. And how bad the wounds are. Time might heal things, but it doesn't necessarily do it fast. You could be waiting years for time to put you right. We lost our parents nearly ten years ago now, but time still hasn't fixed that one. Maybe time can only cure the lesser ailments.

I wondered what had happened to Alain's parents, and if maybe the soldiers had gone back and had done for them when he was abducted. But it wasn't the kind of thing you could ask. Only, if they had, he'd be an orphan too, just like me, and Martin.

I said this to Peggy when we were alone by the wheel, and she looked at me and said, 'Then we're all orphans, Gemma,' which took me aback, as I had never thought of Peggy being an orphan before. You don't think of old people as being orphans. But most of them are, of course. There can't be many one-hundred-and-twenty-year-olds around who're still getting birthday cards from their parents.

Alain was kind of ugly-good-looking. It depended on how you saw him, and the facial scars gave him a sinister, but also a rather distinguished appearance. Sometimes he looked almost handsome; others, when he was brooding and lost in his thoughts, he looked like someone with too much experience of too many of the wrong things at too young an age. You even felt sorry for him then, like you wanted to go and comfort him, but afraid that if you tried he might snap at you and bite your head off.

'You ought to ride that creature or let it go, young man. Look at it,' Peggy said.

Alain was retrieving the crossbow bolt from the target. We all looked back at the sky-fin, which was flying along behind us, looking as miserable as a sky-fin can – which is pretty miserable. But then miserable is their natural expression, so it doesn't mean it's how they feel inside.

The sky-fin was tied to the rail and it flapped along, keeping pace with the boat. It did seem a shame to have it tethered like that.

'You can always tame another one,' Peggy said.

Alain looked at her.

'Easier said,' he mumbled.

'Well, it seems cruel to drag it along.'

'All right.'

He went to the rail and freed the rope, then removed the harness and bridle, patted the creature on its bottle-shaped nose and said, 'There. You can go now.'

But it didn't. Not straight away. It looked bewildered by its new freedom – a bit like a prisoner who unexpectedly finds the cell door open, and wonders if it's safe to make a run for it, or if it's all some kind of trick.

The boat edged away. Finding itself left behind, the sky-fin flew faster, to keep up with us. Then it realised it didn't have to, and it lagged further back. Then, with a sudden whoop, it dived and was off, streaking across the sky, turning and swooping and performing all kinds of acrobatics before it disappeared into the distance, and that was the last we saw of it.

'How about some food?'

It was Peggy's suggestion, but she didn't look like she wanted to cook it, and Martin had got stuck with the last meal, so it was my turn. When I headed for the galley, Alain followed me.

'I'll help you,' he said.

And I was going to say no, but changed my mind and said, 'All right then,' even though the galley was a bit cramped for two. I saw that Peggy was smiling for some reason.

Then, 'Martin, that's enough with the crossbow,' she said. Reluctantly he put it down and Peggy put it away out of his reach, and later on gave it back to Alain, who got edgy when it was too far away.

We went down and got on with the cooking. Alain didn't say much, but he knew how to cook.

'How old are you?' he said at one point.

I told him.

'You look younger,' he said.

It turned out that we were the same age. But he looked older to me. But then he would, after what he'd seen. Sometimes you grow up fast. He told me a little about his family, how they'd lived and where they'd travelled and how he was going to find them again one day.

I wondered then about Peggy and all this schooling that

she believed was going to be the answer to everything. I wondered if that was really it – or all of it. I'd noticed she was getting slower these days, and creaked more when she moved, and you'd catch her nodding off when she was pretending to be attentive and awake. Maybe she was really taking us to City Island because she was getting too old to look after us now. Or even something else, something worse and more final. But then, as I was thinking this, Alain came up next to me and said,

'Watch out, it's going to burn . . .'

I'd been daydreaming and the rice was boiling dry. I reached to take the pan off the heat, and as I did, my arm brushed his. He recoiled, as if he'd been scalded.

'It's OK, I've got it,' I said.

I guess being a soldier makes you nervous.


I think journeys must always have those stretches in them where the world just turns into limbo and time doesn't pass any more and distance doesn't close. You just go on sailing, and the heat haze shimmers and the sky-fish fly by and it could be today or it could be tomorrow, but you wouldn't really know the difference. Even talking's just too much of an effort, so on you go in silence, drifters on the solar tide, and there's nobody else around and only barren deserted islands to keep you company.

We all sat on the deck, under the canopy, keeping out of the sun. Peggy dozed, Martin got on my nerves, Alain sat saying nothing – with us but somehow alone and self-contained. If you wanted a word from him, you had to talk to him first.

Hours and days went by. We crossed the Main Drift. We saw a faraway sky-trawler, then a hospital ship, one which cruised the outer islands, offering surgery and treatment for those who couldn't make it to a city. Then we saw a cruiser, a huge floating hotel, its decks lined with loungers and wrinkly old people.

'Peggy . . .' Martin began.

'No thanks,' she said.

He just grinned at her.

'No one's packing me off on any cruises,' she said. 'I'd rather stick skewers in my head.'

And on we went. Peggy altered course.

'I'm taking the back way,' she said. 'Too busy here.'

She didn't like the Main Drift. She said a boat like ours could get smashed into by a sky-whaler or a factory-ship and be turned into smithereens and no one would even know.

'Be like swatting a midge,' she said. 'We'll take the less-travelled road.'

So we did.


We picked up another thermal and sailed on past some fishing islands. There were sky-trawlers tied up at the harbours, with their nets hanging beneath them like baggy, droopy underwear. These were all small places – the boon-docks, Peggy called them, where people made a living, but only just, and their kids did as they did, and grew up, and went fishing, and had kids of their own who grew up and went fishing as well. I guess they never got as far as City Island or ever caught a school book in their nets. Or maybe they already knew all they needed to survive.

These islands came and went and soon we were lonely again, with infinities of sky and sparse slivers of land. But then, just as I was dozing, I saw Martin getting up and taking the telescope from its holder by the mast. He raised it up and looked through it at an island that was coming into view.

'Peggy,' he said. 'What is *that*?'

I went to the rail to get a look. Even without the telescope I could see them. All along the coast of the small island we were approaching were what looked like scarecrows – huge, crucified scarecrows. There were maybe fifty of them. They stood at least three metres tall, and the span of their outstretched arms had to be two metres wide at least. They'd been mounted on posts, shaped like crosses. It looked like there had been a massacre, but what of and who by, I could only guess. But when I tried guessing, I couldn't.

Alain reached out and took the telescope from Martin.

'Can I?'

'Sure.'

He looked, then handed the telescope to Peggy. He waited until she had looked through it before giving his opinion. That was how Cloud Hunters were – respect for elders – well, when they weren't being soldiers anyway. (Though Peggy said that in her opinion you shouldn't just

123

respect people for being old. They still had to earn it, same as anyone. But then, I guess she'd earned it too.)

'It's a skinner, isn't it?'

'Certainly is, young man,' Peggy said. 'Thought they'd all died out. Not seen a skinner in decades.'

'It's a what?' Martin said. 'What's a skinner? What is it?' And he would have snatched the telescope away, only it was my turn.

'Just be patient, Martin.'

'But what's a skinner? What is it? What does it do? What are those things on the crosses?'

'Skins,' Alain said. 'That's all.'

'But skins of what?'

'I think –' he looked at Peggy for confirmation – 'they're rats.'

'Rats!' Martin said. 'Rats? But they're enormous.'

'Sky-rats,' Alain said.

'Wow! I didn't know they got that big. They're the size of sharks.'

'And bigger. You don't find them everywhere, but in some parts of the sky they're a plague. The fishermen hate them. They mangle the nets and plunder the catches. There's a bounty on them – so much per tail. The government pays. And the skins are valuable. They make fine, soft leather. You'd sell those skins for a small fortune when a trader comes by.'

'Wow . . .'

It was a grim, eerie sight as we sailed along. All those

skins, pinioned and stretched and nailed out to dry. Curious as the view was, we had no intention of stopping.

Yet as we came parallel with the island, a man rushed to a promontory at the shore, and he began to wave and to shout at us. But we couldn't hear what he was saying.

'He looks a bit crazy,' I said.

'Rat-skinning for a living, who wouldn't look crazy?' Peggy said.

'Should we keep going?'

'Rule of the sky,' Peggy said. Which, basically, meant that we had to stop. If someone needs your help, you give it, as you might need theirs one day. That's the rule of the sky – half altruism and half self-interest.

The man went on waving and shouting, looking a bit frantic and afraid that we might just keep going.

'OK. Let's see what he wants. Agreed?'

I nodded, and so did Martin. Alain slightly inclined his head. Then he went and picked up his crossbow, loaded a bolt into it, and cocked the trigger.

# 11

# rat-skinning for beginners

**GEMMA STILL TALKING:**

The man on the shore continued waving as we sailed in, but now there was a big smile on his face.

'Come in, come in. You're welcome, you're welcome.'

And that was when I noticed the odour.

'What is that stink?'

'The skins. That's why they're hung out – to cure them. Takes a while for it to go away.'

'Well, it smells of –'

'Rats?' Alain suggested. And he actually smiled. The first one since we'd met him.

'Come on board, come on board,' the man shouted. We threw him a line and he tied us in. Then we got off the boat and onto the shore.

He was half crazy all right. He didn't just smell like a sky-rat, he'd actually started to look like one. And I'd only ever seen the small ones – not the large variety. He had rodent-like features and his moustache looked more like sky-rat whiskers than anything that normally grew on human upper lips.

'What can we do for you, friend?' Peggy asked him. 'You need something? You got some trouble?'

'I do, I do. Cheese, I need,' he said. 'Have you got any cheese?'

He wasn't half crazy, I thought. The halves didn't enter into it.

'Cheese?' Peggy said. 'Are you serious?'

'I sure am. I need some. You got some? I'll pay you. Name your price.'

'I haven't seen cheese, my friend,' Peggy said, 'in over eighty years. These two kids here have never seen real cheese. I don't know about our cloud-hunting companion –' Alain shook his head. 'You won't get cheese this side of the Main Drift for crime, love or money. I can give you some soya cheese.'

'No, no, no. The rats won't go for it. It has to be milk cheese or nothing.'

'Friend, don't you know your history?'

'I know I need some cheese.'

'They brought a few animals from the old world, and that was all. A lot of them didn't survive and the rest – with a few exceptions – only just. And cattle, well, when did you last see an island with grazing on it? There's two islands I know of with cattle on them and that's it. And even there the feed's grown in greenhouses. Cheese is gold dust, friend. Why can't you just have soya?'

'You don't understand, lady,' the man said. 'It's the rats.'

And he twitched, in a kind of rodent-like way, wrinkling his nose up as if it was a snout.

'Can I go and look at the skins?' Martin said.

'Is that all right?' Peggy asked.

'Help yourself,' the man said. 'But are you sure you don't have maybe just a crumb of cheese? There's a big one out there, a big, big one. Been trying to catch it now for two turnings. Wrecks the nets, eats the catches, even killed a shark – I saw it do it. But I just can't catch him. Ignores all the traps. His stomach's too full and he won't be tempted. Doesn't matter what bait I put out, he won't bite.'

Martin and Alain went to inspect the skins. I reached up and felt one of them. They were surprisingly soft – luxurious, even.

'But he'd take some cheese.'

Peggy looked dubious.

'How do you know?'

'Had some once. Bought it off a trader. They love it. Can't resist. Sky-rats and cheese, like catnip. Talking of which, is that a sky-cat you've got there?'

He'd spotted Botcher, peering over the deck rail, wondering if he should risk stepping off the boat and onto land.

'It is.'

'He a mouser?' the man said.

'He's bone idle,' Peggy said. 'He wouldn't even chase his own tail.'

'Pity,' the man said. 'I could do with a good mouser. I had a mouser but he's gone.'

'What happened?'

'Rat ate him.'

'What rat?'

'The one I'm after catching. Hence I need the cheese.'

'Well, I'm sorry,' Peggy said. 'We'd help you if we could –'

'Wait up,' the Ratter (as I'd started calling him in my head) said. 'You've got no cheese, but you've got kids. How old's the boy?'

'What?'

'The young one?' He was looking at Martin. He and Alain were still wandering among the pegged-out skins. 'Not the older one, he's no good. He's come of age, hasn't he, or he wouldn't have the scars.'

'Why are you asking?'

'Because they like boys.'

Peggy was looking alarmed now.

'Who do?'

'The rats. Like boys. Kids. They like the smell of them. How'd the kid there like to make some money?'

'What was that?'

Martin had big ears when he wanted to have them. You could ask him to do the washing-up and he wouldn't hear you. Mention money and he'd have no problems hearing a pin drop.

'Oh no,' Peggy said. 'I really don't think this is a good idea. I really don't think so. I'm these children's guardian. And I really don't think –'

'Safe, lady,' the Ratter said. 'Safe as houses. No risk at all. We just leave him out on the far shore there, let the wind carry the scent of him, the big old sky-rat out there gets a sniff, in he comes, we plug him, the boy's fine. No worries.'

'No, wait a minute,' Peggy said. 'Just hold on –'

'I want to do it, Peggy!' Martin was all but hopping up and down. 'Let me do it. I want to do it. I've never been rat bait before. How much will you give me?'

'Well . . . I'll give you fifty ICUs, kid. How's that?'

'A hundred!' Martin said.

'Seventy.'

'Now, just hold on, Martin.'

'But, Peggy, you said yourself we don't have much money and you don't know how we'll ever manage when we get to City Island, and I can give it to you for when you go back home, to buy some things for your island, or you can even stay too and not need to go back and –'

'We don't need a hundred ICUs, Martin –'

'But you had to spend your savings on fixing the solar panels, and that was my fault because of the sky-shark and the leftovers. Oh, let me, I want to do it. I've never been a piece of cheese before!'

Martin might have been my brother but I could never quite figure out if he was brave or stupid. Maybe it was a bit of both.

'I'll wait with him, if you want –' Alain spoke up.

The Ratter looked at him and at the crossbow in his hand.

'You good with that?'

'I can use it.'

'If you hit it before I do, I'll give you fifty.'

'We'll see.'

'See, Peggy. It'll be all right. I'll be the mouse-trap cheese –'

'Rat-trap cheese, strictly speaking,' the Ratter said.

'And lure it in, and then Alain and the man'll get it.'

'No problem, lady. No danger. No dramas.'

'Please!'

Well, Peggy was never one to play it too safe.

'We all have to grow up, I guess. If you really want to –'

'I do!'

'And it's safe?'

'Safe as houses. I've caught more rats than you'd believe, lady. Only been bit the once.'

He held up his left hand. I saw he had two fingers missing.

'Oh, now wait, now –'

'It's all right, Peggy,' Martin said. 'It was only a couple of fingers.'

'I like this boy,' the Ratter said. 'Like his spirit. Only a couple of fingers, see. You looking for an apprenticeship there, my boy? Rat-skinning, it's a fine life. No two days the same. Fresh air, your own boss –'

'He's not looking for a career in any rat-skinning,' Peggy said coldly. 'He's on his way to City Island, like his sister here, and our guest.'

The Ratter looked impressed and thoughtful.

'Is he? Are you now? That so? You're travelling to City Island? Well now. Is that a fact?'

'So can I do it, Peggy?'

'Well . . . keep your hands out of the way.'

'We do it now?'

'No time like it. You all follow me.'

And the rat-skinner turned and set off at a good pace towards the other side of the island, and he led us across some rocks and to a high crag, which stuck out into the sky. It was bare and exposed and you could feel the wind blowing.

'OK, young fella,' he said. 'You just stand on the ledge there and think good thoughts and let the breeze carry the smell of you out into the sky.'

'I don't smell!'

'Nothing personal, just like natural odours – just you stand there and let that big old sky-rat get the message. Me and the other young fella here will step down behind the rocks so he won't be smelling us. Then when he comes in and starts circling, we'll have him. Young fella's got his crossbow there, and I've got the old harpoon. Can't go wrong, son. Not a worry. This way, if you would, ladies, all got to keep out of the wind. Don't want that old rat there smelling all of us. He'll get his nostrils all jumbled up and won't know what to do with himself. So, if you would –'

So we climbed back down and hid among the rocks, and there Martin was, up on the crag, looked all pleased and proud of himself, like he was the greatest thing since the last greatest thing – whatever that was.

'Do you think that rat-skinner knows what he's doing?' I asked Peggy.

'He knows,' Peggy said. 'But I'm not so sure Martin does. But then there's more to an education than sitting in a classroom.'

The wind was blowing Martin's hair around his eyes.

'Better get that cut when we get to the island,' Peggy said absently. 'Or maybe I can do it later . . .'

The breeze blew; the sky stayed empty. We sat behind the rocks and stayed quiet. My leg started to ache. Then it went to sleep. Then I got cramp.

I was massaging my calf muscle when I heard the sound.

'Here he comes . . .'

I peered out from behind the rock.

Martin wasn't smiling any more. He was looking like someone who needed two things – to change his mind in a hurry and to go to the toilet in an even bigger hurry than that.

'Oh, my –'

It was massive. It looked more like a bat than a rat. Huge, cloth-like wings, a long head with a protruding muzzle, clawed limbs and a rodent's teeth, and two black, bulbous eyes that seemed on the verge of popping out.

The creature fluttered to a halt and stopped on the ledge, a few metres away from where Martin stood.

'Aren't you going to shoot it?' Peggy hissed.

'Not yet,' the Ratter said. 'Only going to get one shot.

Miss and he won't be coming back. Let him get in a little closer.'

Alain raised his crossbow and took aim.

'No firing till I say, young fella,' the Ratter said. Alain nodded slightly, but didn't reply.

The Ratter loaded his harpoon into the gun.

Martin was looking very white. The huge sky-rat was making peculiar clucking noises, and then it began to sniff, long, deep inhalations. And then it hopped, like some great, black rabbit, and it was only about two metres away now.

'Hadn't you better –?' Peggy whispered.

'It's OK, ma'am,' the Ratter said. 'Years of experience. Know what I'm doing.' And he raised the harpoon gun. But the missing two fingers of his left hand did not exactly inspire confidence in you.

There was a whimpering sound. I thought it was the sky-rat at first. But it was Martin. He was standing there with his eyes shut in complete and abject terror.

'Brave young fella there,' the Ratter said admiringly. 'Don't often get bait brave as that.'

'Shoot the –'

The sky-rat leaned forward and sniffed at Martin's neck. It seemed to approve. It tilted its head sideways, opened its jaws, bared its massive, protruding teeth and –

And then it just fell, sprawled to the ground, with a harpoon in its chest and a crossbow bolt in its head.

'Hope I didn't spoil the skin with that 'poon there,' the Ratter said, getting to his feet. 'Nice shooting, young fella,' he said to Alain.

'I'll just get that bolt back,' Alain said.

'Waste not want not,' the Ratter said. 'Better get my harpoon.'

We walked to where the sky-rat had fallen. Martin was lying next to it. He'd passed out. Peggy went to him.

'Martin . . .'

He opened his eyes.

'Did we do it?'

'Hundred ICUs coming your way, young fella. And fifty for the sharpshooter.'

A smile lit up Martin's face.

'I wasn't scared,' he said. 'Not at all.'

'Martin,' I said. 'You were terrified.'

'A bit,' he said. 'But I still did it.'

The Ratter slapped him on the back and nearly sent him flying off the crag.

'That's the spirit, young fella,' he said. 'That's the real rat-skinning spirit you've got there. Want to watch me gut him?'

'Oh, yeah,' Martin said. 'Can I?'

I left them to it. I'd had enough. I decided to go for a walk.


When I came back, it was all done, and the huge skin was pinioned out with the rest, drying in the sun.

'Come to the house and get refreshed,' the Ratter said. 'And I'll pay you what I owe. And there's someone I want you to meet.'

So we followed him back to his house, which was the

only one on the island. Rat-skinning was plainly a solitary kind of occupation and not to everyone's taste.

'Come in and get out of the sun,' he said. 'We've got water, we've got ice – I make my own, worked out how to do it. Come on in.'

We went inside. The house was small but tidy, and the rooms were shady and cool. He got us drinks and offered us a taste of rat meat, but nobody took him up on it. And then we discovered who he wanted us to meet.

'Angelica! Come down and say hello. There's some folks here.'

There was silence, then the opening of a door and the sound of steps on a staircase, and then into the room came a girl, about Martin's age. She was extraordinarily pretty behind a pair of big, round glasses, and in her hand she carried a book – one that looked very old and dog-eared, as if it had been read many times.

'This is my daughter, Angelica. Angelica, say hello to the folks.'

She looked at us, a little shy.

'Hello . . .'

'We don't see much by way of folks, especially not her age.'

She stared at us with open and even affectionate curiosity, as if children were a strange novelty that it would take her a while to get used to. I noticed too that Martin was staring back at her, as if he even preferred her to the one hundred International Currency Units that he was holding in his hand.

'You like books, young lady?' Peggy asked her.

'Yes,' she said. 'I do.'

'But we don't have but two or three and she's read them over and over. So I was wondering,' the Ratter said, 'if you might do me a favour. That is, seeing as you're going there anyway. And I'm happy to pay, happy to pay, whatever you ask, whatever it needs . . .'

Peggy sighed. I think she could see it coming. She knew what it was going to be long before he said it.

'Would you take her with you, to City Island? She's starved for learning, poor thing, isn't that right, Angelica? And you wouldn't believe the brains on her, and me just a rat-skinner and all. It must be her mother she got them from, certainly wasn't me. But would you? I'll give you all I have. Would you take her? Please, ma'am, would you take her? She'll be safe with you, I know it. Take her with you, please.'

Peggy looked at her and said, 'Is that what you want, Angelica? You want to leave your dad?'

The girl shook her head.

'But you want to go to school too?'

And she nodded.

'Then that's a hard one, isn't it now?'

'I'll come and see you, Angelica. Next turning. I'll fix the boat and save up money and you can show me City Island and tell me all you've learned. You can't stay here rat-skinning – it'll do for me, but you've got the brains –'

She went over to her slightly smelly rat-skinning dad and put her arms around him.

137

'I know, darling,' he said. 'I know. And I'll miss you terrible. But it's what your mother would have wanted too. It's for the best.'

And I knew we'd have to budge up and make a little more room on the deck. Because we now had another passenger to take with us.

One thing did puzzle me though – why didn't the rat-skinner use his own daughter as rat bait? She was the same age as Martin. There were two explanations for that, as far as I could reason. The first was that she didn't smell right for the sky-rats; the second was that he loved her too much and didn't want to risk losing her. But he was quite happy for us to risk losing Martin. And even I thought Martin was worth a little more than one hundred International Currency Units. In some ways, he was quite irreplaceable.

# 12

# angelica

**MARTIN BACK HERE SPEAKING AGAIN:**

Well, Gemma can go and do whatever she likes, whenever she chooses, as far as I care. It makes no difference to me. But I have to say that all this mooning about she started doing got quite nauseating.

I hadn't noticed straight away. But after a while I realised that she was always telling me about what Alain thought, and what his opinions were, and what the Cloud Hunting views were on this, that and the other. And when it came to her turn to do the cooking, it was all, 'Oh, Alain, would you like to help me down in the galley?' – like he couldn't just have taken a turn cooking on his own. And when it was her turn for the washing-up, it was, 'Oh, Alain, shall we do the washing-up together? It'll be so much quicker with two of us.'

But it never was quicker, not with the two of them gassing away down there – though I guessed it was Gemma who did most of the gassing while Alain got saddled with the listening.

It was quite obvious to me what was going on and pretty pathetic as far as I was concerned. But Peggy just sat there grinning to herself, like she'd not had her funny bone so tickled in a long time, but she never said a word. But I thought, well, there you go: Gemma sees the first boy she's come across in eight years (except me, of course, but as anyone will tell you, brothers don't count) and she thinks he's something special just because he's got a couple of scars on his face and a crossbow. But, anyway, if she wanted to go round acting stupid that was her business and not my problem.

But that's not the point. It's Angelica I want to tell you about. I mean, the only girl I'd ever seen since I was four was Gemma, so my idea of girls was bossy, moody, grumpy, argumentative, prone to cheating at card games, bossy again and occasionally given to kicking you when you weren't looking.

Angelica, though – she was nothing like that. She was really quite an eye-opener. She never told you what to do at all, not a gram of bossiness in her, and she never kicked you up the backside on the sly, not once. And as for pretty, well, I mean, she was pretty enough with the glasses on, but when she took them off and blinked at you with those big blue eyes of hers, well, I'd never even imagined anyone could be that pretty. Not that I'm saying Gemma's ugly or anything. She's presentable enough and scrubs up nice and clean, as Peggy would put it, but that's not the same as film star looks. Not that I'd ever seen a film back then, but I'd heard about them. And Angelica definitely had those film star looks with her glasses off.

But I wouldn't want you to go thinking that I'm a soft touch for a pretty face, as I'm not – that kind of thing doesn't count with me at all. No, it was all the things she'd read about and done that interested me. Angelica could remember whole chapters from books by heart, and she had so many rat-skinning stories that you could never have enough of them. She hadn't just sat at home turning pages and looking out of the window, she'd gone with her dad on no end of rat-skinning trips, and what Angelica couldn't tell you about rat-skinning wasn't worth knowing.

I just used to sprawl there on the deck and listen to her, as we tried to pass those long, weary travelling hours. She told me about the time her dad had his two fingers bitten off by a sky-rat, but how they had killed the sky-rat anyway and then gone and cut it open to get the fingers out and see if they couldn't be reattached.

But get this. When they cut the sky-rat open, they didn't just find two fingers in there, they found four – and still in good condition. Which meant the other two had to have been bitten off recently, or they'd have been digested.

So, anyway, then, Angelica said, they set off for the nearest hospital ship to try to see if her dad could get his fingers stitched back on. He knew which ones were his as the other two were a very dark brown, and he was more on the pale-skinned side, so that part wasn't a problem – not identifying the fingers anyway. Her dad could put

141

the finger on his fingers and no trouble. But they never did find the guy who belonged to the other fingers anywhere, which was a pity, as maybe he was looking for them and hoping to be reunited.

But by the time they got to the hospital ship though, it was no good. The fingers were drying out and the skin was shrivelling up like parchment, Angelica said. And the surgeons couldn't do anything, though they offered him a couple of plastic ones. But her dad said it was real fingers or no fingers at all; he wasn't having plastic, as what use were plastic fingers to a rat-skinner? So he'd been two fingers short ever since. And she had plenty of stories like that, lots of them.

So this is why I thought she was someone special and still do. As I have met other girls since, but they never have any rat-skinning stories or have been on any rat-skinning adventures like Angelica had. She really was someone special. And as we sailed along, filling those long empty hours just talking and imagining about things, I used to think how great it would be if me and Angelica could go rat-skinning together one day. In fact, I even asked her.

'Would you take me rat-skinning with you one day, Angelica?'

'I'd love to, Martin,' she said. 'I think that would be great.'

And I'd picture us sailing off rat-skinning together and hunting us down some big ones and maybe even getting our photos taken, with the two of us standing side by side, and some big felled sky-rat lying on the deck. I even thought that one day we could get married and get our own island and set up our own rat-skinning business. But when I hinted at it, she said she was sorry but no, as she was hoping to become a doctor one day. And when she said that I did wonder if it was so as to stitch people's fingers back on when they got them bitten off and other bad experiences.

She said her dad didn't want her going in for rat-skinning, as although it was a good living, it was looked down on, and was on a level with collecting the garbage. Though I don't see what is wrong with either of those things. Rubbish has to be collected and rats have to be skinned and people ought to be grateful that somebody's doing it. She said her dad wanted her to do better for herself, like surgery and being a doctor and so on. But while I could see that being a medical woman was certainly different from rat-skinning, I didn't see how it was necessarily better. But what did I know? And maybe once you got to City Island they taught you why rat-skinning was inferior, and I was looking forward to hearing the arguments and being persuaded against my views.

I asked Angelica what had happened to her mother – if it wasn't a sensitive spot – and whether rats had got her too, not just the fingers but the whole deal. But she said no, it was nothing like that. She said it was the loneliness that got to her, and being on that small island with nothing but two other human beings and a whole lot of dead rats for company, pegged up to dry out in the sun. So one day she had flagged down a passing cruiser and asked for a job on it and hugged them both and said she'd be back. But that was turnings ago and she hadn't been back at all, not even for a visit. So I guess that rat-skinning isn't to everyone's taste, for which, apparently, there is no accounting.

I got Peggy over to listen to some of Angelica's rat-skinning stories, but I don't think she enjoyed them as much as I did, and Angelica didn't tell them so well in Peggy's presence either, like it was cramping her style a touch.

Later on Peggy came over to me, when Angelica was down below doing whatever it is that girls do to keep themselves so pretty, like polishing their glasses and so on, and she said, 'She's a smart little thing, that Angelica, isn't she, Martin?'

'Brain like a factory,' I said, feeling – yet not really knowing why – that I should emphasise her brains rather than her looks.

'You like her, do you, Martin?'

I just shrugged.

'She's got some fine rat-skinning stories,' I said.

'Yeah,' Peggy said. And then added, 'Hasn't she though?' Whatever that was supposed to mean. 'Yeah, she's smart all right,' Peggy repeated. 'And plenty of imagination.'

'Isn't it good to have imagination, Peggy?'

'Sure it is.'

'Didn't you always say?'

'I did, Martin.'

144

'"Just imagine," you used to say. If I ever said I was bored, you'd say, "Use your imagination."'

'I'm not denying it.' Then she looked at me and smiled – which I was pleased to see, as she hadn't smiled much lately and had been looking old and tired, which she maybe was, but hadn't shown it. 'I never thought I'd be taking four of you on the school run,' she said. 'Never imagined we'd be picking up waifs and strays and stragglers along the route.'

'Are we waifs and strays, Peggy?'

She reached out and ruffled my hair, like she hadn't done so much recently, though she did it a lot when I was small.

'We're all waifs and strays, darlin',' she said. 'One how or another.'

'You're not though, Peggy, are you? I mean, you'll always be there.'

'I'll try to, Martin,' she said. 'But listen . . . you know . . . one day –'

'One day what?'

'Oh, nothing. I'll tell you another time.'

'Peggy, what are you going to do when we get to City Island?'

'Well, I won't be joining you at school.'

'Will you be going home again?'

She looked away from me and didn't answer straight away. Then she smiled again – the smile of a thousand wrinkles, as she called it. Her. Not me.

'That's right. I'll be going home. Back to my island and

old Ben Harley – or, should I say, even older Ben Harley – and my smallholding and . . . yup, that's what I'll do.'

'Peggy,' I said, 'you won't be lonely, will you?'

'Of course not, darlin'. I'll be too busy for that.'

'If I thought you were going to be lonely I wouldn't go to City Island.'

'No, I'll be fine. You don't worry about that.'

'And there'll be the holidays.'

'That's right. You can come and see me.'

'How'll we get there?'

'I'll come and get you. Or buy you a couple of tickets on a tramper. Take a while, but you'll get there.'

'Then that's OK, then,' I said, feeling greatly reassured that she was going to be all right without us, for after all, she saved us from being orphans when she didn't have to.

'Here comes the love interest,' she said. Well, I think that was what she said. I didn't quite catch it. And I didn't know what she meant. 'I'm going to check the autopilot, make sure it's doing its job.'

'OK.'

Angelica came back over and joined me under the canopy on deck. Her glasses really gleamed and I could tell that she'd been polishing them, and she smelled nice, like soap.

'Where's Gemma?' I said.

'With Alain, gutting fish for dinner.'

'Huh,' I said. 'No surprises there then.'

'You OK, darlin'?' Peggy called over.

'I'm fine, thank you, Peggy,' Angelica said.

'Good.' Peggy smiled. 'You keep him in order.' Then she went back to looking at the charts.

'She's nice, your grandma,' Angelica said. 'She must be the oldest person I've ever seen.'

'Clean living and whisky,' I said.

'What?'

'That's what she tells people when they ask how she lived so long. Clean living and whisky.'

'What's whisky?'

'Old Ben Harley makes it and puts it in a bottle. He says it's whisky but I think it's more likely drain cleaner. And it's good for deterring midges.'

'You want to play draughts again, Martin? Maybe you'll win?'

'Nah . . . not right now, Angelica. I don't suppose you'd have any more rat-skinning stories, would you? I guess you'll have run out and told me them all by now.'

'No . . . no . . . I don't think so. Just give me a moment to remember some of them now . . . yes, right. So did I tell you about the time my dad and I had this huge great sky-rat cornered, but then the harpoon gun misfired, and Dad had to strangle it with his bare hands?'

'No, you never mentioned that one. I'd like to hear about it, I really would. And all the details. Including the gory ones.'

'Then I'll see if I can remember them all, Martin.'

'Like, did he have to poke it in the eye? Don't leave anything out. Make sure to include the eye-poking if there was any.'

147

'I'm just recollecting and bringing it back to mind to have it ready for the telling.'

'Great,' I said. 'Great. And was there any eye-poking? Or anyone getting any bits chewed off?'

'You know, I think there was that day. In fact, I'm sure of it.'

'Perfect. And you'd better tell me how you gutted it after you caught it too, and whether there were any fingers inside, or maybe a leg or something.'

And I really did think it was special that someone could be so pretty, like Angelica. But not just that – that she could have so many good rat-skinning stories right there at her fingertips and up her sleeves too. I reckon a girl like that could have been an honorary boy quite easy and no trouble. I reckon if I'd found a few more boys and we'd had a vote on it, we'd have let her in straight off, and no arguments. And she'd have had a seat at the top of the table, and the big comfortable chair, with the arms.

# 13

# a small, and unfortunate, explosion

**MARTIN STILL SPEAKING:**

'How long till we get to City Island, Peggy?' I asked, and not for the first time, more for the umpteenth. Or maybe even the umpteenth plus one.

'Not far now, Martin,' she said, which was the standard answer. And she threw the dregs of her green tea overboard. A little shoal of sky-fish pounced on them and snaffled them up.

But I felt she was just trying to keep me quiet. It had been 'not far now' since we set off, and I didn't even know if we were halfway there yet.

'Are we halfway there yet?'

'I hope so.'

'So it's about the same again?'

'Could be, Martin. Kind of depends on the route we

have to take from here. I'm trying to keep to the back roads. Maybe another seven days, maybe ten.'

'OK.'

'You getting bored?'

'Just wondering.'

'Maybe we'll stop off somewhere, get a change of diet and a proper shower.'

You couldn't waste water on a boat like ours, you had one basinful each per day for the whole business, teeth brushing included.

'At least the sky's clear now,' I said. 'Nothing nasty coming our way.'

'Don't speak too soon,' Peggy said. 'Let's not tempt providence.'

But I already had.


We saw them about an hour later. There were so many you could barely count them all, and they were constantly moving and drifting, which made assessing their numbers near impossible. I thought, when I saw them, that it was a swarm of sky-jellies – not the men-of-war, but the smaller, more friendly ones, the ones without the poison sacs. But that was only what they looked like. It wasn't what they were.

Alain advised Peggy to cut the solar engines and close the wind sails. Even she didn't know what they were. But he did.

'They're just jellies, aren't they?' she said. 'They're not going to bother us.'

'No,' Alain said. 'They're mines.'

'What?'

'It's a minefield.'

'How do you know?'

'Wait . . .'

He fetched his crossbow and fitted a bolt into it. Then he went and stood on the prow and fired the arrow high into the air. It arced up and then fell; on its descent it hit one of the 'jellies' – which immediately exploded. The shrapnel from the explosion set off three or four other mines, which exploded in turn, and they set off others, then the noise stopped, and it was quiet again, and we could see pieces of the mines falling down towards the sun.

'Well . . .' Peggy said. 'Well now . . .'

The minefield was huge and the mines were drifting in the wind.

'Can't we go around it?' I asked.

'We can try,' Alain said. 'But it might drift with us.'

'Under it then?' I said.

'We'll lose buoyancy and sink,' Peggy said.

'Over it then?' I was running out of options now.

'Atmosphere's too thin,' she grumbled.

'Go back then, and find another route?' I suggested.

'That'll add more several days, but it's safest,' Alain said.

Peggy looked thoughtful.

'A few more days? I was hoping to get there in good time, before the term started –'

'Or we can try to sail through it,' Alain said. And he and Peggy shared a look.

I stared at the minefield ahead of us. I couldn't say that going through it seemed like a very good idea.

151

As we floated, trying to make a decision, we were hailed by another sky-boat, a smallish one, about the size of ours, which had come out from the shelter of a tatty-looking one-boat island over on our right.

'Ahoy there!'

The boat was steered by a man, bare-chested and sunburnt, with a couple of gold teeth in his insincere-looking smile, and a scraggy beard that hadn't been trimmed lately.

'Ahoy there! You need a pilot? You looking to get across?'

Peggy looked at him like she wasn't too impressed by his character, at least if his appearance was any true indication of it.

'Maybe,' she said.

'I can guide you,' the man said.

'Oh yeah?'

'Taken plenty of boats through. Not lost a one.'

'Oh yeah?'

'Seen a few folk try it on their own – never made it, though.'

'Oh yeah?' Peggy said. 'That so?'

'How many of you?'

'Five.'

'Do it for a thousand Units.'

'*How* much?'

'It's two hundred Units a head.'

'You don't charge by the boat?'

'Charge by the passenger.'

'That sounds expensive.'

'It's the expertise you're paying for. Expertise, know-how, local knowledge.'

Peggy looked more doubtful than ever, and a touch suspicious with it.

'And how'd they get there? All those mines?'

The man shrugged. Peggy scowled at him.

'Didn't plant them there yourself, by any chance?'

'Lady, please –'

'So how'd they get there then?'

'Just drifted in. Some war zone somewhere. They lay the mines then the war moves on and the mines get forgotten about and the solar tide takes them –'

'And they end up by your doorstep and you make a living out of them?'

'It's an ill wind, lady,' the man said, and he showed us the gold teeth again. 'It's an ill wind that don't blow somebody some good. I ain't the only one making a living out of misfortunes.'

'Well, we don't have a thousand Units,' Peggy said. 'So I guess the answer's no.'

'Eight hundred. I'll do you a discount as it's kids.'

Peggy shook her head.

'Friend, if I had eight hundred Units, I wouldn't be giving them to you. And as I don't, I won't be giving them to you either.'

The man chewed his lip.

'Six hundred to get you through. That's my last and best.'

'Well, thanks anyway,' Peggy said.

'OK,' the man said. 'You'd better go round the long way

then. It'll cost you three or four days. But it's your time. If you ain't got money, then time's the alternative. Sorry I can't do it no cheaper, but I'd be undercutting myself, and then if word got about . . .'

And he touched his forelock with his finger, in a kind of mock and sarcastic salute, and he turned his boat around and went back to his scrap-heap island.

'Shyster,' Peggy muttered. 'Wouldn't surprise me if he bought all those mines army surplus and laid the whole minefield himself, just to rip off unsuspecting travellers. Well, I suppose we'd better turn around and go back and take the long way.'

She went to take a look at the sky charts.

'Or I could do it, if you want . . .'

It was Alain. Peggy looked at him.

'You do it? Pilot the boat?'

'Wouldn't be the first time.'

'You've sailed a boat through a minefield?'

'Few times.'

'Have you now? And you got through?'

'Here I am as evidence.'

'Right . . .' Peggy stood, weighing up the chances. 'What happens if we hit one? Will it sink the boat?'

'Not necessarily. It could do. Could trigger a chain reaction with other mines nearby and blow us up. Or it could just be some damage and injuries.'

'What kind of injuries, son?'

'Arms, legs, chest . . . head and neck . . .'

'Oh, *those* kinds of injuries. Nothing too serious then,'

Peggy said. Alain twitched, irritated, but he didn't respond. 'What do you all think?' she asked.

'I trust Alain,' Gemma said. (But, as I may have said before, it was no surprises there.)

'I'm willing to chance it,' Angelica said. But I sort of knew she would be; after all her rat-skinning escapades, she wouldn't be bothered by a few sky-mines.

'Martin?'

'Well . . .'

I wanted to turn around and go the long way, but I was too afraid to say I was afraid. It was the embarrassment more than anything. I wondered then if other people had also got themselves into situations they didn't want to be in, just out of sheer embarrassment and not wanting to be put down as the local wimp.

'Fine by me,' I said.

'OK, young man,' she said. 'You've got the wheel.'

And she got out of the way and let Alain take over at the helm.

'All right,' he said. 'Before we start, everyone get something, a broom, boat-hook, pole, anything. Cover the end with a cloth, something soft. If a mine gets too near, then very gently push it off. But don't, whatever you do, touch the spikes – or it'll go. All right?'

'I think we've got that,' Peggy said.

'All right. Then I'll open up the solar panels –'

He did. And we began to move. I heard a gold-toothed voice calling to us, from the nearby island.

'You'll kill yourselves, you crazy sons-of- –'

But Peggy just yelled back at him to hold his tongue. And on we sailed.

The problem was that they didn't stay still. The slightest thermal, the smallest change in the wind, and they'd drift in a second to somewhere else. The way would be clear in front of you, and then there were suddenly five sky-mines blocking your way, and you had to swerve or dive, or swing around in a moment.

'One coming up port side, Martin.'

That was my bit. Port side, stern. I saw it coming and got the broom to it and gave it a shove.

'Not that hard, Martin!'

The mine veered off, but it gathered speed as it went, and about a hundred metres from us, it crashed into another.

'Get your heads down!'

Alain ducked too.

Next thing, there was a boom, and then shrapnel every-where, and bits of metal embedded in the boat.

'Anyone hurt?' Peggy said. Nobody seemed to be. 'Not so enthusiastic next time, eh, Martin?'

I wanted to say, let's turn around and go back. But, when I looked, the mines had closed in behind us, and going back was every bit as bad as going on, maybe even worse.

Alain turned the wheel to move the rudder, and set the tilts to angle us up or down; we moved on through the minefield, and the mines drifted past us.

'They so look like sky-jellies,' Gemma said.

'Yes, they're supposed to,' Alain told her. And I did wonder if he and the Liberation Enlightenment Army hadn't laid a few mines themselves, maybe even these ones, surrounding us right now.

'Look over there.'

Angelica was pointing to the right, where a pod of sky-whales was bobbing along, heading towards us through the outskirts of the minefield.

'Great Whites . . .'

'Yes, and you know what they eat, don't you?'

'Sky-fish,' I said.

'Yes. Sky-fish. Sky-jellies in particular.'

'Oh dear . . .'

There were six of the sky-whales. It wasn't difficult for them to avoid the mines. A flick of a fin, and they were past. The trouble came when the lead whale got hungry, opened his jaws, swallowed down what he thought was one sky-jelly, and then gulped down another. Then he carried on flying, and they were all coming towards us. And the big whale had two sky-mines inside him.

'Oh no . . . oh no . . .'

Alain took evasive action, steering around more of the mines, but the whales kept coming. Then, without so much as a blink, the lead whale simply exploded, and there were bits of meat and blubber raining down everywhere, all over the sky and the boat and the deck.

'Oh, that is gross . . . that is –'

'All over my sandals!'

'Gemma, you don't need to worry about your sandals right now,' Peggy said. 'When we're out of this minefield you can worry about them.'

'That is . . . disgusting . . .'

It wasn't too pretty, I had to admit. I saw that Angelica was frantically polishing her glasses, so I guess she'd got hit by the exploding whale too. As for the other whales in the pod, they just flew on, oblivious, like they hadn't noticed one of their number was no longer with them.

'They're thinning the mines . . .'

They were too. We were through the middle of the minefield and coming out of the other side.

'Starboard. Three coming up!'

We all rushed to starboard and fended the mines away from the hull. I used the broom gently this time. The mines lazily floated off.

Then finally – and I guess it had taken little more than an hour – we were through. The mines were behind us, and there they stayed, grim reminders of some long-forgotten war or inter-island dispute. The mines outlived the wars and went on fighting them, and inflicted punishments for old enmities on perfectly innocent strangers.

'Do you know what the war was about, Peggy?' I asked.

'All I know is there's always one on somewhere,' she said. 'And everyone says how terrible they are, and how this latest war is the war to end all wars, and how everyone ought to learn from it, and then they go and have another anyhow, like they never learned anything.'

'Maybe they never got educated at City Island,' I said. But she shook her head.

'When it comes to warring,' she said, 'the only difference education has is it makes you better at it, more's the pity.

You think just stupid people fight wars? The generals, the colonels, the admirals, the commanders – educated, every one of them. You know how long it takes to train a professional fighter? They're educated people. If I were you, I wouldn't put too much faith in education when it comes to keeping the peace.'

'Peggy, do you want to take the wheel now?'

We'd forgotten about Alain and hadn't even thanked him. He looked exhausted.

We told him how great he was – Gemma especially. I saw that, like the rest of us, he was pretty dirty and covered in bits of blubber and didn't smell too good. But then, when you've got a sky-whale exploding in the vicinity, what can you expect?

So when I spotted the sign before anyone else did, I was pretty pleased with myself, and gave myself full marks for observation. Because you can have a basin wash on a boat like ours, like I said, but a proper shower and laundry and a meal other than sky-fish are just impossibilities and like mirages in the sun.

But there it was, right ahead of us, with ten or more boats moored up at its jetty: The Inter Island Motel and Skyway Services. Prop: J. P. Procrustes. Food, accommodation, showers, laundry.

I went straight into badgering mode.

'Peggy! Look! Can we stop and get a shower and something different to eat? And maybe sleep in proper beds for a night? Can we? It'd be so nice to have a shower, wouldn't it, and get all these . . . well . . . bits off us.'

'Can you read the room rate?' she said. 'My eyes aren't so good.'

'Says eight Units a room. But we can share. We don't need a room each. And we could have a meal too. A not-fish meal. Can we, Peggy? Can we afford it? Can we?'

'I guess . . .'

'And it looks all right, or all those other boats wouldn't be there, would they?'

'I guess not. Seems to be popular. But then there's not exactly much by way of choice in the area. Only motel we've seen so far in the whole, wide sky.'

'But it's got to be OK. Can we go there? Can we?'

'Well, it would be nice to get a good, long, hot shower and wash these clothes . . .'

And I could tell that though none of the others was saying much, they'd have appreciated a nice long shower too.

'It must be OK if there's other boats there,' I said again, and that kind of clinched it. Peggy was persuaded.

But I was wrong about that – about the place being OK, just because it looked popular. Seriously wrong. Conclusions are things you should go ambling towards; you shouldn't go jumping to them. But I didn't know that at the time.

No. Just because a place looks busy, that doesn't mean it's anywhere you want to be. Appearances can be deceptive, as we were about to find out.

# 14

# motel

Yes, well, so that was all thanks to Martin and his big mouth and wonderful ideas yet again.

Looking before you leap was never his strong point, as he was to prove once more. It's not that he's ever short of suggestions. He's had some classic ones. Like, 'Let's jump off the headland here, Gemmy. I can sky-swim this, no trouble!' And that nearly had us both killed, with him getting into difficulties and thrashing about with all the grace and buoyancy of a dead sky-walrus, and me just about able to keep him afloat and get him back onto solid ground. Even I didn't tell Peggy about that one.

And it wasn't just the motel, to be honest. He'd been getting on my nerves for quite some time, ever since we had the bad fortune to run into that rat-skinner and took Miss Speckles on board. (Least that was how I thought of her, but I kept the nickname to myself.) Not that I had

161

anything against Angelica – she was very friendly and very nice. It was Mr Lovesick who was the pain in the nether regions.

I mean, I know Peggy said it was high time we got ourselves to City Island, and not just for the self-improvement but for the socialising's sake too. She said if we weren't careful we'd end up feral – which meant, according to her small but well-thumbed dictionary, that we'd end up as domestic creatures gone wild and impossible to tame or to let into the house without putting papers and litter trays down first and locking up the biscuits.

'You won't know how to relate to people, not anyone of your own age. And old Ben Harley's no role model, I can tell you that. You need to meet young people and know what's going on with them.'

And I could see the truth and value of that, and I could understand that as Martin had never seen any other girl apart from me (and sisters plainly don't count) since he was too small to even know what a girl was, then meeting one might come as a surprise. But I hadn't expected him to actually start drooling. And when I saw him with Miss Speckles, and when I saw Botcher the sky-cat with a bowl of food, it was hard to tell the difference between them, except that maybe Botcher dribbled less.

Martin just followed her around the boat like she had him on a piece of string, and it was, 'Angelica, shall we do the cooking together?' and 'Angelica, shall we share this watch and both stay awake and then I'll stay awake for your watch too?' Or, worst of all, it was, 'Angelica, have

162

you got any more rat-skinning stories that you haven't told me yet?'

And there the poor girl was, racking her brains for old rat-hunting yarns to keep him happy, and they got more and more unbelievable and far-fetched as we went along, and everyone could see it apart from Martin, who was swallowing them down like they'd been cooked on toast. I did feel quite sorry for Angelica, and knew she was only making them up for his sake. But when we got to the one where she was swallowed whole by a sky-rat and her dad had to pull her out by sticking his arm down the creature's throat and getting her by the hair – well, I thought, even Martin isn't going to fall for this one.

But no. He just nodded like it was something straight from the pages of *A History of the Sky Island Peoples* and as true as the sun shining. I just didn't know where all this rat-skinning was going to end. It was hard to keep a straight face sometimes. But finally Angelica put a full stop to it when Martin was on at her to tell him just one more.

'I really think I've told you them all, Martin,' she said.

'There must be one you haven't told me,' he said. But you could tell she was suffering from creative burnout and liar's block (which is no doubt like writer's block; liars and writers – so Peggy says – being pretty much the same thing, and if you have an aptitude for one, then you may well have a knack for the other). But Angelica plainly didn't want to tell even one more rat-skinning tale.

'No, I'm sorry, Martin. But why don't you tell me about you, and living on Peggy's island?'

'Nothing ever happened,' he said.

'Martin,' I said, 'tell her about the Barbaroons, when they nearly carried you off to sell you – not that they'd have got much, mind.'

'They tried to kidnap you?' Angelica said, all big eyes behind her glasses. She could be as cute as peas sometimes.

'It wasn't that interesting,' Martin said.

'No, go on.'

So he told her. And one story led to another, and just listening to him made me realise that even on a tiny island miles from anywhere civilised, you can have an interesting life. Even a fascinating one, when it comes to recounting it, though it didn't seem so special at the time.

Anyway, so there we were, sailing into the Inter Island Motel and Skyway Services. Prop: J. P. Procrustes. There were pictures up in black and white, silhouettes of rice bowls and chopsticks and one of a bed and another of a shower nozzle flowing, so even if you couldn't read you could still get the message that here was everything weary travellers needed to get the grime and sweat off themselves and the weight off their feet and to have a good tuck in.

'I'm getting a burger,' Martin said.

'They don't do burgers,' Peggy said.

'They do. There's a picture of one.'

'Is that a burger? I thought that meant there was a capstan to tie your boat up at,' Peggy said.

'Ha, ha,' Martin said.

'What's a burger?' Alain asked.

164

But that's the kind of world it is. Nobody knows everything. Sometimes even experience proves nothing.

We tied up with the other boats.

'See, popular place,' Martin said again, like he just couldn't stop with the bragging and the being proved right.

'So you keep saying,' I told him.

'Can you smell cooking?'

'No,' I said.

'I can smell the burgers.'

'In your dreams.'

We walked across the pontoons and up onto land. Then we followed the path to the reception. For a place with so many boats at its moorings, there didn't seem to be a lot of people about. Or any, come to that.

'Where are they all?'

'In their rooms, sleeping.'

'I wonder who runs the place?'

'Ring the bell.'

'Think they'll have any rooms left? They might be full.'

'Ring the bell again, please, Gemma.'

'I'll do it!'

'Ring it, Martin. Not smash it.'

'Yeah, all right, Gemma, keep your hair on. I didn't ring it that hard, did I, Angelica?'

'Well, I didn't think it was that loud, Martin.'

(It really did make you sick.)

'Anyone coming?'

'Here's someone now.'

A woman appeared behind the reception desk. She was formidable-looking, with brawny arms and a tattoo on one of them, of a dagger stabbing a heart and a serpent coiled around it. But she was friendly enough, if gruff.

'Howdy.'

'Hi,' Peggy said.

'Help you?'

'We'd like to freshen up, maybe stay a while, do some laundry, get a shower and a meal – do you have any rooms?'

The woman indicated the key board and all the hooked room keys hanging there.

'You can take your pick.'

'Oh, good. We just thought you might be full.'

'Why'd you think that?'

'The sky-boats tied up at the jetty out there.'

'Oh, them. No. We ain't full.' And she gave no further explanation. 'How many rooms are you wanting?'

'Well, the boys can share, and Gemma and Angelica too, and a room for me.'

'Three rooms, one night, twenty-four ICUs, cash appreciated, in advance.'

'Eh . . . OK. Fine.' And Peggy got her wallet out. 'You've got laundry facilities?'

'Down at the end of the block.'

'Showers?'

'In the rooms. You'll be wanting to eat?'

'I think we will.'

'Meat or fish? The meat we have to get out of the freezer to thaw, so some notice helps. Fish is fresh.'

'Can I have a burger?'

'Sure, young man. We'll get that out of the freezer for you.'

Peggy handed over the money and the woman gave her the keys.

'You manage your own luggage? Don't look like you've got much. Or shall I call Mr Procrustes to carry it for you?'

'We can manage.'

'Going far?'

'City Island.'

'Right. Expecting you there, are they?'

'Kind of.'

'And people at home to miss you too, I guess?'

'No, not really,' Martin blurted out, before I could shut him up. I didn't like this woman. She asked some funny questions. What did she want to know if there was anyone to miss us for?

'OK, well, make yourselves at home,' Mrs Procrustes – I assumed that was who she was – said. 'I'll go and get the meat out the freezer.'

'Where do you get it from, by the way?' Peggy asked. 'I've not seen meat in – well – twenty turnings or more. I mean, old world livestock, that's so rare – and expensive.'

'Mr Procrustes knows the people to get it from,' she said, and then clammed up, like it was some trade secret.

'OK. Then let's get freshened up, shall we?' Peggy said, taking the keys and doling them out.

'You know, you all don't smell so good,' Mrs Procrustes said. 'And there's bits of fish or something on you.'

'We realise,' Peggy said. 'It's why we want the laundry and shower.'

'What happened? You smell like a whale exploded.'

'Something like that,' Peggy said.

'Then you carry on. When do you want to eat?'

'Couple of hours' time suit everyone?' Peggy asked.

It seemed to. So we went to our rooms.

# 15

# frozen dinners, chilled meals

**GEMMA CONTINUING HERE:**

Miss Speckles was OK really. It was the first time I'd talked
to her properly on her own, but she was fine to share a
room with.

'My brother annoying you, Angelica?' I said. 'I can speak
to him, if he is.'

'No,' she said. 'He doesn't annoy me at all.'

'Not even with the rat-skinning stories? I thought you
might be feeling the pressure.'

'No, really. I don't mind. In fact, I quite like him.'

So there you are. Just when you think there's no surprises
left in the world, some girl tells you that she likes your
brother.

I wondered what he and Alain were talking about
across the corridor in their room. Martin was probably
putting the squeeze on him to relate a few crossbow-firing

stories, or floating-sky-mine stories, or being-press-ganged-into-the-army stories. I just hoped Alain would tell him the truth and frighten any notions out of him of one day being a soldier himself.

'Beds aren't very big, are they?' Angelica said.

I tried mine out.

'No. Bit short.'

'Maybe they might change them.'

'Could mention it.'

'But then you curl up when you sleep.'

'You want the shower first, Angelica?'

'No, you go.'

So I did. Then she did. Then we put on some clean clothes and took the mucky stuff to the laundry area, where we found the others.

'I've still not seen anybody else,' Martin said. 'Have you, Alain?'

'No, no one.'

'Where are all the owners of the boats?'

'Sleeping?'

'But none of the other rooms seem occupied.'

'Stretching their legs?'

'Maybe. But all of them? And it's not that big an island. You'd think we'd see somebody.'

We got our clothes washed and hung them out in the sun. They dried fast, long before the time we'd agreed to eat.

'I really can smell those burgers now,' Martin said.

'You've been smelling burgers since you were born,' I told him.

'That and your far—'

But Peggy managed to stop him.

'That's enough, Martin. Thank you very much.'

'I'm going exploring,' Martin said. 'You coming, Angelica?'

He would have asked me once. But I was happy to stay with the grown-ups.

'OK.'

Off they went together.

'Don't be late for dinner.'

Peggy said she was going to rest. I walked on with Alain round the coast. We all went rolling and waddling. We'd been sailing too long and hadn't got the knack of the land again yet. We ran into Mrs Procrustes, who was there on the headland, throwing garbage into the sky.

'It all falls into the sun,' she said. 'So it's not littering.'

But half of it wasn't heavy enough and just floated away on the thermals.

I thought I'd mention the beds.

'Is it possible to get a longer bed, please, maybe?' I said, politely as I could. 'Mine's a bit short.'

'The ones in our room are the same,' Alain said.

Mrs Procrustes looked at us, as if sizing us up.

'Beds too short?'

'A bit.'

'Legs hanging over the end?'

'A little.'

Then a big smile opened up her, so far, rather sullen face.

171

'Not a problem. I'll get Mr Procrustes to step round after supper, and he'll be only too happy to sort that matter out for you.'

'Thank you.'

'Just need to have a bed more your size, huh?'

'If possible.'

'Or, I guess, if you were a little shorter, that might help as well – huh? Like if you stopped at the ankles or something?'

And she patted us both on the shoulder and we made an effort to join in the joke and laugh along with her. But I didn't think it was that funny.

'Weird woman,' I said, when we were out of earshot. Alain nodded.

'Yes,' he said. 'But most Islanders are weird – to a Cloud Hunter.'

'But is that what you still are?' I said.

'Always,' he said. 'Forever.'

I felt he might have said something more, or even done something more, as we were alone together for the very first time and there was nobody else around –

'Gemma! Gemma! Gemma! Gemma! Gemma!'

Yeah. Exactly. Always there to spoil my treasured moment. Mr Bigmouth running for all he was worth (which wasn't a great deal) across the escarpment, followed by Miss Speckles, who was shouting, 'Alain! Alain! Alain!'

They didn't so much stop as collide.

'Gemma. Gemma. Got to get Peggy. Got to get out. Get Peggy. Get our things. Get out. Now. Right now. Now!'

172

'OK, hold on. Where's the emergency? Just slow it down.'

'We've got to get out. Now!'

'Martin, we haven't eaten yet,' Alain said.

'And I thought you wanted a burger.'

'No!' Martin yelled. It was nearly a scream and I had to clamp my hand over his mouth. He bit it.

'Ow!'

'No, Alain . . . Gemma – Angelica and me – we saw inside the freezer.'

'What were you doing nosing about?'

'We were round the back and the kitchen door was open and there was no one there, so we went in, and I wanted to see what was in the freezer.'

'So?'

'So Angelica kept watch by the door and I opened the freezer.'

'And?'

'You know we thought it was funny that all those boats were tied up, but there's no one around –'

'What about it?'

Martin moved his mouth but no sound came out. He looked appealingly at Angelica to speak for him. It came out straight and level and somehow flat.

'They're all in the freezer,' she said.

I said the most ridiculous thing. It just came into my head.

'But aren't they cold?'

And then I realised what an absurd remark that was.

173

'They're not cold, Gemma,' Angelica said. 'That is – they are cold – but they're not feeling it.'

'And you know we were talking earlier about the beds being a bit short.'

'Yes?'

'I think I know how they fix the problem.'

'Yeah. Give you a longer bed,' I said. 'We just asked her about it.'

'No, Gemma. They don't make the bed longer. They make the person sleeping in it shorter.'

'But that's impossible,' I said. (More ridiculous, not-quite-getting-it remarks.) 'To make someone shorter, you'd need to cut their feet off and –'

And then I saw Angelica's and Martin's faces staring at me.

'They're all in the freezer,' Martin said. 'We counted ten pairs, plus an odd left one on its own. And a shoe.'

I looked at Alain.

'And I left my crossbow in the room,' he said. 'Come on. Let's get Peggy.'

He ran. And we followed. We didn't stop until we were banging on the door of Peggy's room and telling her to open up. Alain dashed to his room to get the crossbow.

'Can't a one-hundred-and-twenty-year-old get five minutes' sleep?'

'Peggy, open the door.'

She did. Finally.

'What's the problem? And can't it wait?'

'Peggy, grab your stuff, put your sandals on, we've got to go –'

'What? We've only just –'

'Peggy!' Martin was yelling again. 'There's people in the freezer! And feet!'

And then there was silence. We all had our backs to the corridor, all except Peggy, who was looking out from her room. She kind of tensed and stiffened.

'Oh my –'

I looked around.

They were both there. Mrs Procrustes, from reception, and with her an ugly, boiled-face man, who looked as mean as a thousand Scrooges. He had one good eye, and in his right hand he carried a cleaver, and in his left one, a meat hammer. He faced us and said:

'Who's complaining about the beds?'

'Well, as a matter of fact I –' Martin started. But I got my hand over his mouth.

'Actually,' Peggy said, 'you don't need to worry about them. We've decided to leave early. Everyone – shall we go?'

'But my toothbrush – I've left it in –'

'I'll get you a new one, Martin. Everyone – go!'

We headed down the corridor, pushed open the fire exit and ran.

'What about the laundry?'

'Grab what you can.'

We snatched what we could off the line on our way past and went on running. Alain and I took one of Peggy's arms each, to help her keep up. We made it as far as the jetty, our hands full of laundry and belongings, all flying

175

in the wind. The couple of monsters were still coming in pursuit.

'Go on ahead,' Peggy said. 'Untie the boat.'

I did. Alain, to give me cover, stopped and loaded his crossbow, took aim and shot the cleaver right out of the man's hand. He let out a roar, bent to retrieve it, and started after us again. Mrs Procrustes meantime was coming down the jetty and over the pontoons like an unstoppable tank. And that was what did for her: she couldn't stop, and when I tripped her, she just kept going, out into space. I heard the yell, but I didn't hear the landing or the sizzle – but then, it is a very long way down. And it's not everyone who has the knack of sky-swimming. Some people never really learn.

'Come on. Get on board!'

The ship was untied and the solars were open and the other three were already on. We jumped across a gap of space and made it. Behind us the cleaver kept on coming, with Mr Procrustes firmly attached to it.

'You'll pay for this! You'll pay for this!'

'We already have,' Peggy reminded him. 'Twenty-four International Currency Units. And I never got my night's sleep.'

In a fit of rage – or maybe it was pique – he hurled the cleaver. It spun through the air and landed with a vibrating thud in the deck.

Alain pulled it out.

'Might come in handy for something,' he said.

'I'd prefer not to keep it on board, Alain, if you wouldn't mind. Considering what it's been used for,' Peggy said.

'Oh. Yes. Take your point.'

I thought Alain was about to drop it over the side. But he didn't. He just threw it back with all his might, towards the man who had hurled it at us.

I don't think Alain meant for it to happen. It was just an unfortunate thing. Because the cleaver could have landed anywhere. But it landed where it did. And it was hard to feel any sympathy for the man lying back there on the pontoon.

'Martin, Angelica – don't look,' Peggy said.

Only, they already had.

'I don't think that was a very good motel,' Martin said as we got under way.

I was about to give him a major ticking-off for that – and then I saw from his face that he was being perfectly genuine. It wasn't sarcastic, it wasn't knowing, it wasn't even an attempt at a joke. He was completely serious. He did not think it was a good motel.

'I'm not staying at one again,' he said, 'if they're all like that. What about you, Angelica?'

Sometimes I'm just grateful I'm not Martin's age any more. But I'm positive I was never that bad. Surely not. I couldn't have been. Or maybe I was. One day I'll have to ask Peggy. Or, then again, maybe I won't.

# 16

# troubling thoughts

**GEMMA JUST ROUNDING THIS PART OFF:**

So on we sailed. When you've somewhere to reach, what else can you do? You just keep on moving and moving gets you there in the end.

I liked the travelling, but I had mixed feelings about the getting there. I didn't know if I was going to like City Island or not. And what was going to happen to Peggy? Was she really going to turn around and go home, and make the whole journey back on her own?

Meanwhile we carried on with the usual routine, taking turns with the cooking and cleaning and keeping watch. Or we took a turn at the helm and got the hang of reading the sky-charts. Because one day everyone has to make their own way around the world, and it helps to know which direction to sail in and how to read the good signs and the bad omens.

One late watch, when I was up by the prow, and everyone

else was sleeping – or so I thought – I heard this stifled sobbing noise, and when I went looking I found Angelica hiding away, rolled up in her sleeping bag by the stern.

'Angelica – are you all right?'

It took her a while to emerge, but when she did she said, 'Gemma, I'm homesick. I miss the island and I miss my dad, and I know you'll think it's stupid, but I miss the sky-rats too.'

I sat down and put my arm around her. She was shivering, but it wasn't from cold.

'I don't,' I said. 'I don't think it's stupid at all. I miss home too, and it wasn't much, just a rocky island with a few bits of green, but I miss it like I had toothache.'

'It's not that I don't want to go to the big island and go to a school . . .'

'I know.'

'I just miss everyone.'

'I know. And everyone does. We all miss people.'

She stopped crying and wiped her eyes.

'Do you miss your dad?'

'Yes, I do. And I miss that I never really knew him, nor our mum either. We were both so young when we lost them. I can barely remember them or picture their faces. I don't know if Martin can remember them at all.'

I realised then that there was something else rolled up by the sleeping bag with her, and Botcher's fat face appeared.

'So this is where he goes.'

'He sleeps next to me. I don't mind.'

'Good. You'll stop him from feeling lonely.'

'That's what I thought. Gemma –'

'Hmm?'

'How can you miss someone you never really knew?'

'It's like a hole, Angelica, like a great big hole in you that nothing can ever fill. And it doesn't really matter how nice and how kind other people are, that hole's always there. You don't always think about it; it's not that you're sad all the time – it's just that you know it's there. And people who don't have that hole in them, they don't really understand . . . but someone else who does – you kind of recognise them . . .'

'Like you and me!' she said. 'We're sensitive, aren't we, Gemma?'

'Yes,' I said, to keep her happy. 'We are. I think there's a secret society of people who've got holes in them.'

'And Martin too,' she said.

Which was news to me.

'Really?' I said. 'Martin?'

'Yes. He misses your mum and dad really badly.' And of course he must have. But we'd never really talked about that, even though we were brother and sister. We'd never spoken about it at all. 'He told me,' she said. 'And I said I understood.'

'That was good of you, Angelica.'

'And you can talk to me too, Gemma, if you ever feel sad.'

'Thanks,' I said. 'I'll maybe do that. You going back to sleep now?'

'I'll try.'

'OK. Goodnight then.'

'We say goodnight but it's hardly ever dark.'

'Put on your sleep mask.'

'I will.'

I gave her another hug and left her. She wasn't so bad. And you don't feel so bad yourself when there's someone you can comfort in some small way. Though maybe all you are really doing is comforting yourself by feeling useful and wanted.

I went to the helm and checked the charts and the auto-pilot, then completed the remainder of my watch. Alain took over from me, and I lay down and slept. When I awoke everyone was up and moving and fish were frying in the pan. There were a few sky-crab catchers in the offing, who waved as they passed us by. Then we were in empty sky again for a while, with islands in the distance beckoning us on.

And then I heard Martin's voice from across the deck, repeating one of his favourite phrases.

'Peggy! What is *that*?'

And looming down from above us was the most extra-ordinary craft I'd ever seen. It was shaped like a long, cylindrical tube and didn't have a single porthole in it. It appeared to be flying blind, and whoever was inside it – if anybody was – couldn't be seen.

'Peggy – do you know what that is? Have you seen that before?'

181

'I've seen pictures of them.'

'What is it?'

'They used to be called submarines.'

'It's a USO,' Alain said. 'Never thought I'd see one, but it's a USO.'

'What's a USO?' Martin asked.

'Unidentified Sailing Object,' Angelica told him. 'My dad sees them all the time.'

'Yes, and so does old Ben Harley,' Peggy said. 'Especially after a session with the private stash.'

'Where's it from? And what's it doing here?' I said.

The thing was heading for us and it slowly came alongside.

'How can it see where it's going? Where's its eyes?'

Just as I said that, part of the roof opened and a long swivelling pipe came out, with a gleam of glass at the end of it, and it turned itself around until it was pointing directly at us. And then it stopped.

'Are there people in there? Or does it do that all on its own?'

'There's someone in there,' Peggy said. 'But they can't be like us.'

'Then where are they from?'

'Up there, I guess,' she said, and she pointed up at the myriad distant islands that floated above us in the upper atmosphere.

'And they've come down here? What for? To gawp at us?'

'The spirit of scientific enquiry, no doubt.'

'So you mean there are – well – aliens up there?'

'I suppose that would be one word for them.'

'So it's an alien sky ship?'

'More or less.'

'They're not going to abduct us, are they?' Martin said. 'And stick probes up our –'

'Martin –'

'Noses.'

'Don't be ridiculous. Where did you get that from?'

'One of Peggy's old books.'

'So why are they hiding in there?'

'The atmosphere and the heat here would probably kill them,' Peggy said. 'We couldn't survive at their level, and they can't live at ours.'

'Shall I wave at them?' Martin said.

'How do you know waving means the same to them as it does to us? Waving could be extremely rude to them for all we know – a provocative gesture – even a declaration of war,' Alain said.

'Well, I'm going to risk it,' Martin said. 'I'm going to wave. I don't see why you have to assume that aliens are nasty and out to get you.'

'You were the one going on about the probes,' I reminded him.

'I'll take a chance.'

He waved at the sky-sub's periscope as the vessel floated by. The lens stared at us, and then the front of the sky-sub tilted, and down it went to greater depths.

'Look, it's diving! I'd love to go down there, wouldn't you? Wouldn't you like to go exploring?'

'Martin, you haven't even explored this level yet, never mind the depths.'

'I caught an ugly-fish once,' he said. 'On a two-kilometre line. Pulled it all the way up. Had a face like a bag of lumps, didn't it, Peggy?'

'It wouldn't have won too many beauty competitions.'

'Skin like you wouldn't believe. Ten times as thick as ours, to keep the sun off.'

'What did you do with it?' Alain asked. 'You threw it back, I hope?'

'Well, I would have,' Martin said. 'But it died first.'

'Probably the sight of you that killed it,' I said.

'The sight of someone round here . . .' Martin said, looking pointedly in my direction.

'It's too cold for them,' Peggy said. 'And the air's too thin. The shock killed it.'

'But we gave it a decent send-off,' Martin said.

Alain didn't say anything in reply. I don't think he approved. Cloud Hunters don't like waste. He leaned over the deck rail and watched the sky-sub disappearing. Its rudder spun and down it went, until we could no longer properly see it, and it was just one more speck in the sky, inclining towards the heat of the sun.

'Peggy –'

'Not now, Martin.'

'No, Peggy –'

'I've got to navigate.'

'No, Peggy, what's that? Please.'

'What's what, Martin? What is it now?'

'Over there. On that big island we're coming to. What's that?'

We were just turning out of the deeper sky and re-crossing the Main Drift. Here some big islands lined the way, like houses down a street, but set far, far apart.

Visible on the island nearest to us was a huge gleaming structure, glistening in the sun.

'What is it, Peggy? What's it for?'

'It's a stadium,' she said. 'That's what it is.'

'But what's it for? What do they do there?'

'They play games.'

'What kind of games?'

'Games that people like to go and see.'

'People go and see games? I thought you played games.'

'You do. But some players get really good at games so people like to watch them playing.'

'But what do they play? In a big place like that? What do they do? Alain, what do they play there?'

'I don't know, Martin. Football, probably, I would guess.'

'Football? What's football, Peggy?'

Alain straightened up from peering over the hull. He turned and looked at Martin with an expression of total disbelief on his face.

'Are you serious?' he said. 'You cannot be serious.'

'What?' Martin said. 'What's the matter? Have I done something wrong?'


I met Peggy's eyes. She just sighed and turned the wheel and we changed course for the island.

'OK,' she said. 'We'll go and look at it. But just look. And not for long. I suppose it's all part of broadening the mind.'

'And I do need a new toothbrush,' Martin said.

So we headed in to Football Island (which is what I had christened it, whether that was its name or not – though it turned out to be right.) And it looked as if we had picked the right time too, for the jetty was busy, and the streets were teeming with people, and there was music and singing, and half of the population seemed to be dressed in red and the other half in blue.

And every single one of them appeared to be heading for that big stadium in the centre of the island.

'Does that mean there's a game on?' Martin said, as we sailed into harbour.

'Looks that way.'

'Then we might be able to see it!'

We tied up and got off the boat and hurried to join the throng. But no sooner were we mingling with the excited crowds than I realised that everyone we saw was staring at us. We were walking among them like five sore thumbs. Everyone else was in red or in blue. We were the only ones without affiliation or visible loyalty, the only ones without a team.

# 17

# game on

Gemma said she just wanted to turn around and get out of the place as it was making her feel uncomfortable with all the crowds and everything, but I didn't see why we always had to do what *she* wanted. I wanted to stay and look around, because it was amazing.

All the people. I'd never seen so many.

'Where do they all come from, Peggy? All these people here?'

'You'll cover biology and reproduction at City Island.'

'Is City Island as big as this?'

'Bigger.'

'With more people?'

She laughed.

'Martin, this is just a drop in the sky.'

'Well, I don't like crowds,' Gemma said.

187

'Me neither,' Alain agreed. 'I like individuals. Not masses.'

'I might go back to the boat.'

'Oh don't, Gemma – I mean, you can if you want . . .' Peggy said. 'But let's look around. Just for a while. It's an experience.'

Well, the crowds were everywhere, and all heading for the huge stadium, and it was impossible not to get swept along, like a piece of flotsam on the solar tide. The currents of rippling red and blue took us with them.

'Hey, where's your shirt, kid? Where's your colours?' someone called to us.

'You've got to be visitors, right?' someone else said. 'Where you from?'

'You come to see the game, have you?' the first man asked. 'Well, why wouldn't you? Football Island's famous across the whole system! People come from all over, huh?'

And they were all so proud of their island and so pleased with what went on there that I daren't open my mouth to tell them that up until a short while ago I had never even heard of football, never mind Football Island. I didn't want to sound like an ignoramus.

'Pies, pies, get your pies!'

'Hot drinks! Get your hot drinks here. Chilled ones in the freezer.'

'Souvenir programmes!'

The swelling crowd swept us along past street traders and stalls. The traders were all dressed in team colours too, and the blue-shirted traders got blue-shirted customers, but not a single red one.

'Armbands! Shirts! Coasters! Key rings! Pennants! Flags!'

'Team pictures! All your team pictures!'

'Signed photos of Genaldo! Guaranteed genuine!'

'Who's Genaldo, Peggy?' I asked as we walked by. A man in a blue shirt overheard me and started to laugh.

'Hey, you hear that? Did you hear that? The kid don't know who Genaldo is! The kid ain't heard of Genaldo!'

And everyone around him within earshot – people in red shirts as well as blue – all began to laugh along with the man, and they looked at me until I was as red as the red shirts, and some of them even pointed me out to their own kids, and said, 'How's that for ignorant? The boy doesn't know Genaldo!'

Then somebody turned to Peggy and said, 'Hey, granny – you in charge of these kids here? Well, you're not doing right by them. You want to see they get clued up. Fancy not knowing who Genaldo is. Shameful.'

'Yeah, fancy not knowing that,' someone in a red shirt agreed. 'That'd be like asking who Stellingham is. That'd be unbelievable.'

'Who is Stellingham?' I said. 'I don't know him either.'

Whereupon the man let out a long, low whistle.

'My, oh my. Have we got some ignorance here? Are these kids growing up stupid or what?'

'The world's bigger than your little island and what goes on in it, my friend,' Peggy told him. 'Maybe you ought to teach your own kids something along those lines.'

But the man was already gone, hurrying to join his

friends, who had started up singing a chant of some kind as they moved on towards the stadium.

'*Reds! Reds! Alive or dead! Reds are winners! Reds! Reds!*'

No sooner had their voices died on the air than the blue-shirted supporters around them picked up a chant of their own.

'*Blues are best! Blues are best! Blues are better than all the rest!*'

And on they all went, and on we followed. They were all chanting at once now, each group of supporters trying to drown out the others, but unable to. It was as if exactly one half of the island supported the reds and the other half didn't.

'Peggy, what makes you a red supporter rather than a blue one?'

Before she could answer me, another passer-by butted in.

'Hey, don't you people know nothing? Don't everyone know that the port side of Football Island is red jerseys and starboard side's blue? Don't the whole world know that? Cheeses! Where you been keeping the kid all these years?'

Peggy just kept her temper, shook her head and I heard her mutter, 'No point in arguing with the ignorant. Especially the ones who think they know something.'

The passer-by was a woman this time. She had on a blue shirt, which looked a couple of sizes too small.

'Excuse me,' I said. 'So does that mean if you move from

one part of the island to another you have to change your team?'

She looked shocked.

'Whoever would do a thing like that, boy?' she said. 'Why, that would be turncoat treachery of the worst kind. You'd be shunned by your own family to do a thing like that. I never heard of such a suggestion. Who's been putting notions like that in your mind? They should wash their mouths out. And why aren't you wearing your shirt?'

'Don't have one. We're just visiting.'

'Visiting or not, you should still be dressed properly. Or it's disrespectful.'

At that she strode off, kind of haughtily, like she'd somehow snatched the moral high ground away from right under our feet and was now marching away with it, leaving us without anything solid to stand on.

'Why are they all so . . . fired up, Peggy?' Gemma said.

'You'd have to live here to know.'

'But I mean – if all it depends on is which side of the island you're born – that's just so random, an accident of birth, right? I mean, if you'd been born a kilometre away, you'd support the reds instead of the blues. Or vice versa. Why are you supposed to care so much, all over a little bit of geography?'

'Maybe not everyone does. Perhaps they just put their shirts on and go along with it for an easy ride.'

'Get your hats! Get your scarves! Get your banners now! All your badges! Get your rosettes!'

The current of people was still bearing us along and the high walls of the stadium were getting nearer.

'Peggy, I want to go back,' Angelica said. 'I don't like all the people.'

'Just take my hand. I don't think we can turn back now, darlin'.'

And she was right. There was no way we could have turned back to the boat. There were thousands of people pressing us on. Soon the turnstiles were visible ahead. People were forming into two lines to go in – Reds to the left, Blues to the right.

'Hey, you there. You people. You strangers!'

A man in uniform called us over.

'Here! Step out of the crowd!'

He beckoned us aside to where he stood, sheltered by a pillar.

'Where you going, friends?' he said.

'We wanted to see the game,' I said. 'We've never seen one. We want to go inside.'

'Not dressed like that you're not,' the official said. 'It's Blues one end, Reds the other. Where do you think you're going to sit?'

'Can't we sit in the middle?' Peggy asked.

'Middle? There is no middle. There's no halfway or sitting on the fence here. It's Reds or it's Blues. You've got to choose a side. You can't go in there with no colours. There'd be outrage – could start a riot.'

'Then . . . Blues –'

'Reds, Peggy!'

'Does it matter, Martin?'

'Just thought red looked nicer.'

'Red, blue, I don't mind.'

'Then you need to get your shirts on.'

'We don't have shirts.'

'Follow me.'

He led us towards some lockers at the back of the pillars.

'Keep them here for visitors,' he said. 'Courtesy of the city. There you go. Bring them back, would you, when the game's over?'

He handed us five musty-smelling red football shirts.

'You get many visitors?' Peggy said.

'A few. Not so many. But then, we're a long way from the next football-playing islands. It's a two-week journey at the very least. We don't get many other teams coming.'

'So who do you play?' Peggy said.

The official looked puzzled.

'Who do you think? Reds play Blues. Blues play Reds.'

'What, every week?'

'Twice a week. Wednesday nights. Saturday afternoons.'

'They play each other? Over and over?'

'Hey, it's Football Island, lady. It's how we do things. If you don't like it here –'

'No,' Peggy said, 'we love the place. Just trying to find out a little more about it. How much are the tickets?'

The official looked perplexed once more.

'How much? It's free. You just go in. It's all paid in the taxes. Why, it's a citizen's civic duty to attend all matches.'

Peggy pulled her football shirt on over her head. She

looked kind of funny, an old lady in a football shirt. But then I must have looked funny too, as my shirt was so big it was down to my knees.

'Tell me,' she said to the official. 'Do you have any religions on this island?'

The man narrowed his eyes.

'We have football, lady,' he said. 'That's what we have. We have football and we have the finest stadium this side of the Main Drift and the whole Southern Sky Line.'

'It's certainly something,' Peggy agreed, looking up at the high walls and the statues of, no doubt, famous players, and a great sculpture of a football perched on a plinth. 'It reminds me of a cathedral –'

'It's famous throughout the whole sky world,' the official said proudly. Though up to a short while ago, I'd never heard of the place.

'OK. Just follow the other folk in the red jerseys there,' the official directed us. 'You'll find a seat. Plenty of room for everyone. And enjoy the game.'

'Thanks. We will,' Peggy said. 'Or we'll try, anyway,' she added, when the man could no longer hear her.

So in we went, following the stream of red shirts to the left and then up into the banked stands of the stadium. It was immense, a great theatre of a place, with a band on the pitch playing music and cheerleaders twirling pom-poms and throwing batons into the air, while vendors prowled around selling drinks and snacks and programmes and souvenirs. We found seats and sat down. None of them were reserved. You just took any ones that were free. No matter where you sat the view would have been terrific.

Up on a huge scoreboard were some facts and figures.

THIS SEASON'S RESULTS TO DATE:

BLUES: 6 WINS REDS: 6 WINS

DRAWS: 6 DRAWS

I nudged Alain, who was next to me.

'Alain – you see that? All the results are exactly the same. They're neck and neck for everything. I bet that doesn't happen often, huh?'

But he just looked at me like I was pathetic.

But how was I to know?

The stadium filled and the partisan chanting and singing and flag-waving began. Before I knew it, I was up on my feet too, and waving a flag someone had given me, and I was chanting along with all the other Reds supporters.

It was great. I mean, I didn't know what it was all about exactly, but just standing up shouting and waving your flag was tremendous. Angelica was on her feet too. But Peggy and Gemma and Alain just sat there, and they even looked a bit glum. I mean, I felt that they were letting the side down a bit, to be honest, and they could at least have tried harder and demonstrated where their loyalties lay.

Then the Blues started singing, across on the other side of the stadium. So we started chanting again and we drowned them out. And our cheerleaders, down at the front, were going wild.

And then the teams came on, running out from different

195

entrances but at exactly the same time. And other chants went up. The Blues began it.

'*Genaldo! Genaldo! One in the net. One in the net.*'

While the people in red around us sang: '*Stellingham! Stellingham! Does what no other striker can!*'

And then the game seemed about to start.

Before it did, a singer appeared down on the pitch, and the band struck up a kind of anthem, and the players bowed their heads, and everyone in the stadium stood up, both Reds and Blues, and they all sang a song about what a great place their island was, and how lucky they were to live there.

And then the band and the singer left the pitch, and the teams took their positions, and the referee tossed a coin, and then the captain of the Reds took a short run up and kicked the ball, and the game was under way.

# 18

# two halves

**MARTIN STILL RECOLLECTING THE FACTS:**

Well, the noise was unbelievable. The shouting, the cheering, the klaxon horns, the rattles, the chants, the stomping, the stamping, the jeers, the cat-calls. It was totally awesome. Tides of red and blue rippled in waves. Up on their feet and back down again. Some of the crowd even spelled out the word BLUES with their blue caps. Then on our side the crowd spelled out REDS with their flags.

And down on the pitch the game went on like wildfire, with the players tackling and running, or falling down in apparent agony and with terrible injuries, only to be tended to by men running onto the pitch with sponges and buckets, to help the hurt players back to their feet, and soon they were running about as good as ever.

There were outrageous fouls and tackles and the crowd shouted their disapproval until the referee awarded a penalty. (The Blues were far dirtier players than our team.)

And then there was all the tension and excitement of the penalty shot. And before you knew it, we'd scored one, us, the Reds. And everything just erupted then, and had there been a top to the stadium it would have blown right off and gone sailing away.

The Blues were pretty quiet when that happened and they looked sick as sky-dogs at the fact that we were one up and they were one down. And then the referee blew his whistle and it was half-time before you knew it, and I couldn't believe the game was half-over already, the match had just gone so fast. Gemma was sitting there yawning. She must have been tired.

'It's great,' I said. 'Isn't it? Aren't you enjoying it? I think we're going to win today, you know. Shall we get some snacks?'

But before I could persuade Peggy to buy some, a man sitting behind us, who must have overheard what I said, snorted with derision and said, 'Don't be stupid, kid. We're not going to win today. Where are you from, boy? Planet Stupid? We won the last game. So it's the Blues' turn to win today, then it's a draw the next time, so we aren't due to win until the game after next. Don't you know the basics? I mean, have some sense, kid, will you? Try and keep up.'

I went a bit cold. If what he was saying was right, that meant it was all a fix, a show. It wasn't a real game at all, just people pretending. I mean, if the outcome was a foregone conclusion . . .

'But that's not fair,' I said to the man. 'That means it's all . . . fixed.'

The man looked at the five of us in our ill-fitting shirts.

'Who are you? You all out-of-towners or something?'

'Something like that,' Peggy said. 'Out of somewhere.'

'Well, mark the kid's card then, lady, so he don't sound like some kind of dilly when he opens his mouth in public places. Reds win, then Blues win, then it's a draw. OK? Unnerstand?'

I didn't.

'But – what's the point in watching if you know how it's going to end?' I said.

'What's the point in living, kid, if you know how it's going to end? You still go along for the ride, don'tcha?'

But I didn't want to see any more. The game seemed pointless now. I just wanted to leave.

'There's only ever three outcomes anyway, kid,' the man went on, waxing philosophical (as Peggy used to put it). 'Win, lose, or draw. That's all it ever is no matter who's playing who. Someone wins, someone loses, or it's even. Someone goes home happy, someone goes home disappointed. Then things change, and it's the other way round for a while. Luck comes and goes, then it comes back again. So what's the difference? What's the odds? This way you get all the fun and none of the trouble. Blues win, then Reds win, then it's even stevens and a draw. And everybody's happy.'

'I want to go, Peggy. I don't want to see any more.'

'They won't let you out, kid, not till the end. Not unless you're ill. Or expecting a baby. And I'd say you're not.'

'Peggy?'

'It's not all that long, Martin. We'll just have to stay.'

But all I felt was tricked and disgusted.

I didn't stand up or cheer any more. The second half started and the Reds scored a second goal. But five minutes before the final whistle, the Blues scored. Then they scored again from a penalty. Then thirty seconds before the whistle, they got the decider. But it looked to me as if the Reds' goalkeeper had just let the ball in. It was as if he had deliberately dived one way when the ball was going the other.

The blue side of the stadium went wild, while the Reds got to their feet with a kind of silent resignation and headed for the exits.

'Not to worry,' I heard a Reds supporter say to his friend. 'We might beat them next time.'

'Yeah,' his companion said. 'Or if not, the time after that.'

'Yeah. You've got to stick with your team through the good and the bad, the lean times and the fat, thick and thin.'

'That's right. Some you win, some you lose.'

And they went on their way. We followed them out.

The Blues were happy as babies. They milled around the stadium whooping and cheering. But next week, I thought, they'd be more subdued, when the draw came. And after that, they'd be the disappointed ones, as then it would be the turn of the Reds to win.

It just all seemed meaningless.

'Why do they do it, Peggy?' I said. 'Why?'

'Because they don't have anyone else to play except each other, I guess. And if they did it any other way, they'd probably end up killing each other. But turn-about keeps the peace and maintains the status quo. And anyway, it's only a game.'

'But it ought to be fair. People ought to be trying. Or what's the point?'

'You've got me there, sweetheart,' Peggy said. 'I may be old, but I don't know all the answers. Or even all the questions.'

'It's not like a game at all,' I said. 'It's just a show, isn't it? They're just putting on a show. And all the cheering and excitement and being happy when your team wins and sad when they lose, it's just phoney. It's not real.'

But the people in the blue shirts around us went on singing and celebrating. One of them saw us taking our red shirts off to return them, and said, 'Take it off, kid. I would if I were you. Guess the best team won today. You go and nurse your sorrows, son. Just learn to be a good loser, eh?'

'But you only won because it was your turn,' I said. 'You weren't the better team or anything –'

But he'd gone, carried away in a swarm of blue shirts, and the cheers and the cat-calls moved away from us and the stadium.

We gave the official the shirts back.

'Should have chosen blue, huh?' he said.

'Why?' I said. 'What's the difference? I mean, really. There is none.'

'You come back any time now, folks,' the official said cheerfully. 'Always a welcome for visitors at Football Island. Next match Wednesday evening. Should be a good one too, I hear.'

I couldn't see what would be good about it.

'Peggy –'

'I know. You need a new toothbrush.'

We found a shop and went in.

'Red toothbrush or blue toothbrush?' the lady behind the counter said.

'I'd like a green one,' I said.

'Red or blue?'

'Don't you have any other colours at all?'

'Does this boy have some kind of learning difficulties?' she asked Peggy.

'Quite the opposite,' Peggy said.

'Then what's he talking about? This is Football Island. It's a red toothbrush or a blue one or you don't brush your teeth. So what's it to be?'

'Give us one of each,' Peggy said. 'Always good to have a spare.'

So she bought me a red and a blue toothbrush.

'Now, that's a weird one,' the lady at the counter said.

Peggy gave me my brushes.

'Thanks. I'll use them turn-about,' I said. 'So neither of them feels left out.'

Peggy just laughed and put her arm around me.

'Marty,' she said. 'I'm going to miss you.'

And it really hit me then that she was going to leave us when we got to City Island, and she wouldn't be with us any more.

'I'm going to miss you too, Gran,' I said. 'I really am.'

'Come on, let's go back to the boat and start sailing. It's an education just getting to City Island, huh? Wouldn't you say, Marty?'

'I never thought it would be,' I said. 'But I'm learning.'

'Me too,' Peggy said. 'Even at my age, there's always something new – I'm glad to say. If there wasn't, it might be kind of tedious. But it never was with you two around. I guess you kept me lively. That's something kids are good at – right? – keeping you fresh and up on your old toes.'

# 19

# show me

'*Come on you Blues! Come on you Blues!*
  *Blues, Blues, it's all good news –*'
'*Reds! Reds! Reds we say.*
  *Reds live to fight another day –*'
The shouting and celebrating and the commiserating gradually faded behind us and we left the citizens of Football Island to all their tomorrows. It seemed funny that they'd go on and on doing what they did, playing endless games of football, where the result was never in doubt. And it would never be any different. Some days your team would win, and some days they would lose, or draw, and you would be happy or sad accordingly, and so it would always be.

It's always strange when you're travelling, because your days are changing and varied, while the days of those you pass, or leave behind you, go round like wheels, in patterns and habits, and things that were done yesterday are all to

204

be done again tomorrow. And when we got to City Island, our days would be spinning wheels too.

'Martin!' Peggy called to me.

'What is it?'

'Come over here a moment.'

I went and joined her at the helm.

'What's up, Peggy?'

'Take the sky-charts and show me where we are.'

I did.

'Now show me where City Island is and how you'd get there.'

I did that too.

'I thought you just got Gemma to do this,' I said. 'I overheard –'

'I did. I want to be sure you can find the way too.'

'Well, I can.'

'Good.'

'Why?'

'And you can use the solars, can't you? And you know how the sails can be hauled in or hoisted, and how to tack and all the rest?'

'You've shown me plenty of times.'

'OK. Just wanted to check.'

'Why?'

She was starting to worry me.

'Because a crew ought to know. I just wanted to be sure you can sail the boat – you know – if anything were to happen . . . or if I wasn't here.'

'But – but why wouldn't you be here, Peggy?'

'It's just standard procedure, Martin.'

'Well, I know.'

'OK, well, just to get some practice in, you take over.'

'What – now?'

'Yes, now.'

'Oh . . . all right. What are you going to do?'

'I'm going below. I'm going to lie down a little while.'

'Are you all right, Peggy?'

'Of course I'm all right. Just a bit tired.'

'OK.'

'Just stick to the course we're on.'

'OK.'

That was what I said. But I didn't stick to it. The captain has to use his or her discretion and respond to unforeseen circumstances as he or she deems fit.

Angelica saw it before the rest of us.

'Martin . . . Gemma . . . Alain – look over there.'

In the far sky, about two hours away from us and off to our starboard, was a great bank of cloud. The upper part of it was wide and deep, and must have stretched for a couple of kilometres. But the bottom of it was narrow and swirling, the vapour twisting like a whirlwind and disappearing into nothingness.

'What's doing that?' Angelica said. 'Something's sucking it up.'

'There's a boat there, inside the cloud,' Alain said. 'It's a Cloud Hunter. Has to be. They've got the compressors on and they're gathering it in.'

'Wow – isn't that amazing. I've never seen –'

Alain didn't let Gemma finish.

'Change course,' he said. 'We've got to reach it before it goes.'

'Change course?' Gemma said. 'But we're already running late and Peggy –'

But I think she didn't want to find the cloud-hunting boat because she was afraid it might be the last she would see of Alain.

'Yes, well, I've got the wheel,' I said. 'I've been left in charge.'

'So what? You're not the oldest.'

'What's that got to do with anything? Why does being older give you any more right –'

'Martin, will you change the course – please?'

Which was quite decent of Alain really. He could have just fetched his crossbow and pointed it at my head. But I'd already decided to do it. It might be his own parents in that boat. We couldn't just sail on by. I turned the wheel and opened up the solars to max and got the others to help me put the spinnaker out, and in a couple of minutes we were running full tilt, and you could hear the sound of the wind whistling past your ears – and that was the sound of us moving.

'How far do you think?' I said.

Alain squinted.

'They're two hours away.'

'That's what I thought,' I said, glad to have my estimate confirmed.

'Can we go any faster?'

'No, everything's flat out. It's an old boat. Don't want it falling apart.'

He went to the prow and stood at the rail, watching the great cloud bank grow smaller as the unseen compressor sucked it down.

'Look – there –'

The lower vapour had cleared and we could see the cloud-hunting boat, and the great cloud was now half its original size and shrinking rapidly.

'Fire a flare, Martin, so they can see us.'

'If you like . . . you do it.'

He fired one of the emergency flares into the sky. But I don't think they saw it. They were still an hour away from us, and no doubt engrossed in their work.

'Let me fire another.'

'Alain, there's only one left,' Gemma said. 'What if there is a real emergency?'

'This is a real emergency!' he snapped. But he didn't use the last flare. He left it in the case.

The cloud was going. It was just wisps and traces now, and then it was gone, all folded up and packed away and turned into water in the compressor tanks. And the cloud-hunting boat then raised its sails and opened its solars, and away it went, skimming off on a thermal like whoever was at the helm was a sky-sailor in a race.

'That is some going . . .'

We didn't have a hope. Even if we'd had a faster, more streamlined boat, I didn't have the skill to sail it in that way, and I didn't think anyone else on board did either.

'I'm sorry, Alain, we're not going to be able . . .'

He could see it was pointless. He turned away from the prow and nodded at me.

'Thanks anyway,' he said.

Then he went below.

Peggy appeared a while later.

'What are we doing here?' she said. She knew at once that we weren't where we should have been. 'Are we lost already?'

'We saw a cloud-hunting boat and I had to take a detour.'

'Oh. That's why he's upset.'

'We couldn't catch it.'

'I see. Have you recalculated the course?'

'Me and Gemma did it. It's better if we go this way, rather than sail all the way back to where we diverted.'

'Show me.'

I showed her the new route on the chart.

'It didn't look dangerous. It avoids the Forbidden Isles as much as we can. The only islands we come really close to are these.'

'Oh. The Friendly Isles? We're going that way?'

'Yes. I mean, they sound all right. You're not going to get any problems sailing past an archipelago called the Friendly Isles, are you?'

But Peggy just sighed.

'You kids still have a lot to learn, don't you?' she said. 'See, this is what worries me. I only have to go and take a little nap, and it all starts getting complicated.'

## 20

# friendly

**GEMMA TELLING IT AS IT IS:**

I could see that Martin thought that I didn't want Alain to reach the cloud-hunting boat, but that wasn't so at all. I did. I was praying we'd get there before it finished with the compressors and took off. Why would I ever want to stop him being reunited with his family or getting news of them when I know what it's like to lose people you love? I don't know how Martin could have thought that. I'd never be like that. It's his age still, I guess – just a bit callous, and judgemental.

But I forgot about it soon. Peggy took over at the wheel and I went and leaned on the rail of the boat, next to Angelica, and we watched the so-called Friendly Isles come into view. And when I saw them I soon lost all my worries, for they were the most beautiful places I had seen. But it wasn't only that, they smelt wonderful too; a sweet scent of flowers came from them, fresh and clean, borne on the breeze, enticing and kind of beckoning you in.

'Peggy, what's the lovely smell?'

'Not what you might think. It's kelp.'

'Kelp?'

'Sky-weed. There. One of the rarer varieties. This is the only place it grows, far as I know. Never been found anywhere else. Won't grow anywhere else, though people have taken cuttings and tried to transplant it. Only grows here. No one knows why. Something in the air, maybe – the climate, the rock . . .'

And there it was, fields of it, floating offshore. It didn't look so attractive, but it did smell delicious. And when you inhaled its odour, it kind of went to your head, and made you feel refreshed and happy, and your worries looked far away.

'Peggy, can we stop off and visit the Friendly Isles?' I asked.

'No, sorry. We can't.'

'Ah, Peggy –'

'Please, Peggy –' Angelica joined in.

'Come on, Peggy –' I pleaded.

Alain came back up on deck, and he wanted to visit them too.

'No. We don't have the time. We've wasted enough.'

'But Peggy, just for an hour –' I said.

'Yeah, only it never is an hour. There's people went to spend an hour on the Friendly Isles and they're still there fifty years later.'

'Why didn't they leave?'

'I'll tell you one day. But right now we're not landing to find out.'

211

'But, Peggy –'

'No. Answer's no. What's the answer?'

'No?'

'You got it.'

So we all lined the deck – except Peggy, who kept a firm hold of the wheel – and gazed at the stunning and magnificent Friendly Isles, whose cliffs were adorned with kelp blooms and flowers, and there was even a waterfall, trickling water out into the sky.

'Peggy – they've got water to waste.'

'It's recycled. It just goes round and round.'

I felt that we were sailing past paradise. Why go to City Island, I thought, when there were places like the Friendly Isles, and you could tie your boat up there and rest a while, or even be happy there forever? Whereas studying might end up giving you troubling thoughts and making you unhappy.

'Peggy –'

'No, Gemma, and that's final.'

So that was that. Or should have been.

Only it wasn't.


'Ahoy! Ahoy, please! Ahoy . . .'

Voices called to us from a stationary boat that we were approaching. The two people on board were running up a distress flag too – though it wasn't exactly an emergency they had on their hands, not strictly speaking, not an oceanic one anyway.

'What do *they* want?' I heard Peggy muttering. 'If we

get any more interruptions, by the time we get to City Island the school'll be shutting up for the next round of holidays.'

'Could you help us, please?' a voice cried.

'Hell and damnation,' Peggy said to herself.

'Are we going to pull over, Peggy?' I asked – knowing the answer.

'I suppose . . . Let's see what they want. Sky-cat overboard or something trivial like that, I wouldn't be surprised.'

And she gave Botcher an evil look as he got under her feet, but he took the hint and scurried off out of the way.

'Ahoy, there. What's your problem?'

We drifted in. I threw a fender over so we didn't bang into each other. The boat was a nice one, modern and sleek, and the couple on it looked affluent and prosperous. The sails were spotless and the solar panels gleamed as if brand new. But the boat wasn't going anywhere. It had a couple of sky anchors out.

'You broken down?'

'No, no – we're waiting. We don't know what to do.'

'What's the matter?'

'It's the islands there –'

The man on the boat pointed towards the largest of the Friendly Isles.

'It's our son. We were headed for City Island, to take him to boarding school for the first time, to get educated –'

'Small world, small sky,' Peggy said. 'Coincidences everywhere.'

213

'And we were running early and we came past the islands here and decided to take a look –'

'You went on land?' Peggy said.

'Yes – we just meant to stay an hour or so –'

'OK. Did you eat the kelp?'

'Sorry?'

'The kelp. They cook it, and chew it, and put it into most of their food. Did you eat it?'

'Well, no, we didn't have anything. But our son, Leo –'

'He had something to eat?'

'He said he was hungry.'

'Oh my,' Peggy said. 'Oh my.'

The man looked at her. The woman with him was getting tearful.

'We can't make him come back,' she said.

'No,' Peggy said. 'You wouldn't.'

'He just won't come with us. Just refuses. He says he doesn't care about anything any more. He just wants to stay where he is.'

'Which is where?'

'He's sitting in the park there, with some others his age –'

'And when you tried to make him go with you?'

'The island people wouldn't let us. They got outraged. Nobody can be forced to leave the island. They can leave of their own free will any time they choose. But they can't be made to. Not even if they're under age –' the woman said.

'Especially if they're under age, so that policeman said, remember?' the man interrupted.

214

'Oh my,' Peggy sighed. 'Don't you people read the International Sky Hazards documents before you start sailing places?'

'Well, we did. Of course. I mean, we avoided the Islands of Night, and the Forbidden Isles and –'

'Didn't you read the advice about here?'

'Well – this place is friendly. Isn't it?'

'Oh yeah,' Peggy said, with an edge to her voice. 'Real friendly. Too friendly.' And she sighed again.

'So what is it with this place?' the man said. 'It looks harmless. What's the danger?'

'The kelp,' Peggy said. 'That's why no one leaves. They chew it all day long, and add it to their rice, and garnish their sky-fish with it.'

'It's a drug?'

'Well, there's something in it that makes you happy, all right. Makes you happy, knocks out whatever ambition and motivation you once had. All you want to do is lie in the sun and chill out with your friends and do as little work as possible.'

The man actually looked interested – tempted, even.

'And what's the downside?'

'None, if you don't mind being a mindless zombie the rest of your life,' Peggy said.

'James,' the woman reminded her husband, 'we are trying to get Leo to school. We want him off that island and on our way. We don't want to be there with him.'

'Yeah, well you do have a problem there, don't you?' Peggy said. 'Because if he goes on eating the kelp – and

215

he will – he won't ever want to leave. And the islanders won't let you make him. So all you've got is persuasion, far as I can see. That's the only tool in the box.'

'We spent hours talking to him. He just says, "Mum, Dad, chill out."'

'Chill out?'

'That's right. We've tried everything. Nothing works.'

'Tried abduction?'

'Yes. We tried picking him up but he just starting kicking and everyone around came to help him – and we were told to leave him be or quit the island.'

'Well, you're lucky you didn't eat the kelp too,' Peggy said. 'Or you'd all be living happy and brainless ever after.'

'Might have been better if we had,' the woman said ruefully. 'At least I wouldn't be worried sick right now. Is there anything you can do to help us?'

'Would if we could, but I don't see how we can,' Peggy said.

And then the couple spotted Martin.

'How about your boy there?' the man said. 'He looks our son's age.'

'And what about it?'

'Maybe he could talk him round. He might listen to someone his own age. Or maybe he could persuade our Leo to take a walk with him down to the harbour, and then once he was on the jetty –'

'Bundle him on board and away?' Peggy said. 'That the plan?'

'What do you think?'

I thought it stank. Not nicely, like the kelp. Just stank full stop. What if something went wrong? What if Martin got into trouble? He might have annoyed me at times, but he was my brother and I didn't want to lose him.

'I think it's a bad idea,' I said. 'I don't think that –'

But I didn't get to say any more. Martin was on the case.

'I'll rescue him,' he said. 'I'll do it. Let me, Peggy. I'll do it. Really. I know just what to say. I'll ask him to come to the harbour to go sky-swimming – or to play football –'

'Football?' the woman said. 'You can play?'

'Yeah, sure,' Martin said. 'I know all about it.'

'Don't let him, Peggy,' I said. 'Don't let him do it.'

'I think Martin's being really brave,' Miss Speckles Angelica said admiringly – which didn't really help, as it just fired Martin up to even greater and more reckless feats of would-be heroism and stupidity.

'I might even be able to drag him to the harbour if he won't come willingly. I can knock him out and put him on my back – fireman's lift.'

Leo's mother looked dismayed.

'We don't really want that . . .'

'Only as a very last resort,' Martin said. 'Can I, Peggy? Can I?'

Peggy just sighed.

'I'm getting too old for this,' she said. 'It's a rock or a hard place every single day. Wrong if you do and wrong if you don't. Gemma?'

'I say no.'

'Alain?'

'I'm happy to go instead. But I'm older . . .'

'I think someone Leo's own age would persuade him better . . .'

'Angelica?'

'I think Martin's really brave.'

'OK,' Peggy said. 'Majority has it. Sorry, Gemma.'

'Then I want to go with him.'

'Martin?'

'As long as she stays out of my hair and doesn't interfere.'

'OK. You go together then. And remember, once you're on the island, whatever else you do –'

'Don't eat the kelp,' I said. 'Got that, Martin?'

'Of course I have. I'm not stupid, you know. I'm hardly going to eat the kelp when I know what it does to you, am I?'

Which was true enough. And he didn't eat the kelp either.

He went and did something else just as bad instead.

## 21

# maybe even too friendly

**GEMMA CONTINUING:**

I have to admit that it was hard not to be seduced by the Friendly Isles. They were so welcoming, so enticing, so nice.

I guess that there are people like that too. Everyone tells you how wonderful somebody is, and what great charm they have, and that you can't help but love them when you meet them. So you think – not me, I'm not falling for it, all these charmers are just phonies underneath, and I'm not going to like them at all. But then you meet whoever it is, and you find yourself falling for them too. Well, the Friendly Isles were like that: somehow, you couldn't help liking them and going under their spell, like someone sitting in the hypnotist's chair, feeling heavier and heavier, with your eyelids slowly closing.

'We'll wait for you here,' Peggy said. 'You go and find their son, and talk him into coming down to the jetty, then if we can get him on board and down below, we'll slam the hatch on him and take off, and deliver him back to his parents.'

Their boat was still anchored way out off shore. Peggy thought that if their wayward son Leo saw his parents' boat at the jetty then he'd simply turn tail and run for it. And she was probably right.

'OK,' Peggy said. 'He's your age, Martin – dark hair, red T-shirt, navy shorts, sandals, answers to the name of Leo, last seen in the main square park. You go and persuade him to take a walk to the harbour with you. I don't know what you're going to say –'

'I'll think of something, don't worry. I'm good at making things up and –'

'And lying –' I couldn't help but add.

'Embellishing –' Martin said.

'Yeah, well, you could call it that, I suppose,' I said.

'I can do this on my own, you know,' Martin said.

'Yeah, I know. But I'm still coming with you. Mum's last words to me –'

'I know.'

'*Look after Martin.*'

'Yeah, well, I can look after myself now.'

'OK, so I'll come and watch you do that.'

'Is that the squabbling over for now?' Peggy said. 'Short truce, maybe?'

'Come on then,' Martin said. 'If you must.'

So we hopped down from the boat and onto the jetty and headed into the town of Friendly, capital of the Friendly Isles – and it certainly lived up to its name.

'And remember,' Peggy called after us. 'Don't eat the kelp. Whatever you do.'

'We won't,' I said. 'Don't worry.' And I knew that I wouldn't. But as for Martin . . . well . . .

There was a sign by the harbour, a big town sign in bright colours and with flowers growing around it.

WELCOME TO THE FRIENDLY ISLES, it read, and under-neath it someone had scrawled, SO FRIENDLY EVEN THE GARBAGE DOESN'T WANT TO LEAVE.

I exchanged a look with Martin, and we walked on towards the town.

'Howdy!'

'Howdy, young lady, young man.'

'Hey – strangers. Nice to see you.'

'Hey there, youngsters. How are you? Looking good today.'

Everyone was just so friendly. I'd never met so many pleasant and smiling people, ever. They were all so warm and welcoming, so happy-looking and kind, you just felt at home from the second you arrived. In fact it was like you had lived there all your life, and every single inhabitant was an old friend.

'Friendly, aren't they?' Martin said, as we walked into town.

'Yeah, too friendly,' I said, still trying to keep my cynical defences up, but that was more to impress Martin than anything. Truth was, my defences were being eroded. Why had Peggy told us there was anything wrong with the Friendly Isles? The place was lovely.

There were people working, but no one was working too hard. They all seemed to take life at a leisurely place, and there was time for a break, and a chat, and a word with your neighbours and a talk with your friends. And then, when a stranger came along, it was:

'Hey there, youngsters, how are you this fine day? Now there's a pretty young lady.'

'There's a handsome young man!'

And they were half joking with you, but you felt there was no real harm in it, and that at root they really meant what they said, and were nice as people could be.

On we went.

'Which way is the city park, please?' I asked a passer-by.

'You after seeing our beautiful city park, young lady? Well, you won't be disappointed. You just keep straight on, take a left at the T, go along, left again and you can't miss it. And you enjoy it. There's music there and always plenty of young people and things going on. You enjoy.'

'Thank you.'

And on we went.

'This is a nice place, isn't it?' Martin said. 'Don't you think? I can see why Leo wanted to stay.'

'Yes, me too . . .' And, although I was nearly completely seduced by the island, a little cold, hard part of me was still thinking, What's the catch here? Where's the downside? Where's the reality?

Because I can't believe that anywhere's perfect, nor that

life can be so easy, no matter where you are. There's always a fly in the soup or an insect biting. Life can be good, but it can suddenly turn nasty on you. And while it's nice to stroke the soft fur coat of some lovely wild animal, it's also a good idea to know where its teeth are, in case it decides to bite. And, in my experience, life can bite you at any time, without warning, and it can tear out a big chunk and leave you bleeding.

'I like it here,' Martin said. 'And can you smell the food? I'm getting a bit hungry.'

'You heard what Peggy said.'

'I know. It's just, it smells nice.'

It did too. There were food places everywhere – cafes, street stalls, restaurants. Rice and Kelp. Kelpie Burgers. Sky-fish in Kelpie Batter.

'It looks like kelp with everything,' I said. And it did. And I noticed that almost everyone who wasn't actually eating was chewing.

CHEWS, a sign by a stall read. TEN CHEWS FOR TEN CENTS.

'Shall we get some chews if we can't eat anything?' Martin said.

'Martin, what do you think is in them?'

'I don't know.'

'Kelp, of course.'

'How do you know?'

'What else would it be?'

'We could try one.'

'No. Come on. Look, there's the park.'

223

I began to see the cracks in the jigsaw then. Certainly the people were friendly, and certainly they looked happy – or at least content – but they were happy and content in a sort of empty, glassy-eyed way, like there was nothing special they wanted to do with their lives, and there never would be, just as long as they could have another chew or eat another kelpie burger.

And as I looked around, I could see that things weren't quite as perfect as they had first seemed; the buildings were faded and crumbling and in need of maintenance; things needed washing, bins needed emptying, and the island's children – who you'd think would have been at school – appeared to be at some endless playtime. And while some of them were running around playing, others looked listless and bored, as if they had nothing to keep them occupied other than to unwrap another chew and put it into their mouths.

'Look – that must be him.'

We stopped by a bench. Lying on the grass a short distance away was a group of young people, some my age, some Martin's. Among them was a boy in a red T-shirt, who was sprawled on the grass, his eyes closed, his face in the sunlight, as he listened to someone picking a slow tune out on a four-stringed guitar.

'What do we do?'

'I don't know. But you'd better be subtle about it, Martin.'

'Subtle's my middle name.'

'If it is, it's a recent addition.'

224

'Look, you wait here and give me a few minutes. I'll go over and just kind of sit down and get chatting and then persuade him to come for a walk or something . . .'

'To do what?'

'I'll think of something. Just give me twenty minutes or so then come back.'

'You sure?'

'Two of us go over, he might get suspicious.'

'OK. I'll walk around and then come back.'

'Twenty minutes or so.'

'All right. I'll see you then.'

I watched as Martin strolled off to join the group of people gathered on the grass. He sat and stretched out. Then he saw that I was still by the bench looking at him, and he gestured with irritation for me to go. So I did. Against my better judgement. And I went to look around the town, intending to return in about twenty minutes' time.

But I have to confess that I got a little distracted and wrapped up in the sights and sounds of Friendly, and maybe the casualness got to me too, and I thought to myself, well, where's the rush, what's the hurry? And at one point, before I realised what I was doing, I found myself sitting at a little outdoor cafe, and the waitress came over with the menu and said.

'Hi, how are you, honey? And how are we having our kelpie today?'

Which brought me back to my senses, and I quickly got up, and mumbled something, and hurried on my way – and

I could feel the waitress standing, staring after me, though I didn't look back. And then I got a little lost too, down one of the myriad back streets of the souk, and there were street stalls everywhere, selling food or jewellery, and there was some kind of smoky haze in the air, and I began to feel listless and aimless, and then even forget where I was and what I was doing there.

It was only when someone pushing a handcart nearly ran me over that the adrenalin shock of reaction brought me back to my senses. And I saw on a nearby clock that over an hour had passed, and so I hurriedly retraced my way to the park.

At first I couldn't find Martin. But then I saw him. He was lying in the sun with his shirt off, there among the other young people. And though I walked straight towards him, he didn't seem to see me. He was next to two girls and a couple of other boys, one of whom was Leo, who we had come to rescue, while Martin was trying to pick a tune out on the guitar.

'Hey! It's Gemma! Hi, sis. Come and meet my buddies.'

*Sis?* I thought. *Buddies?* What was this?

'Martin –' I said.

'This is my buddy Leo and my buddy Sam and my buddy Anna and my buddy Theresa and –'

'You seem to have acquired a lot of buddies since I've been away, Martin,' I said.

'I have, sis. Everyone's just so friendly. Why don't you sit down and chill out and take it easy?'

'Martin,' I said, getting him by the elbow. 'Would you

just walk over here with me a moment? I'd like a quiet word.'

He shook my hand off.

'Hey, don't poop the party, sis,' he said. 'Chill out. We're all chilling here.'

'Well, let's just chill over there for a minute, if you wouldn't mind.'

He handed Leo the guitar.

'Here you are, Leo, old buddy. You get some good vibes out of that. I won't be long.'

'Take it easy, dude,' Leo said. Then he glanced at me. 'I like your sister, man,' he said. 'She's a looker.' And he blew me a kiss. Which I thought was damn cheeky.

I got Martin out of earshot of his buddies and propped him against a tree.

'Martin –'

'Why the long face, sis?' he said. 'Hey, lighten up, here. Where's the fire?'

'Martin, what did Peggy tell you? What did I tell you?'

'Don't eat the kelpie, sis. Do not eat the kelp.'

'Exactly. So how much have you had?'

'Me? None. No, no, no. Not a kelpie morsel has passed my non-kelpie lips.'

I didn't believe him.

'You sure?'

'Cross my die and hope to heart.'

'Cross your heart –'

'And hope to die. Right.'

'You've eaten nothing?'

'No.'

'You're sure?'

'Positive. Nothing at all. I just had a drink, that was all.'

I groaned.

'What did you have?'

'Juice.'

'Where from?'

'The stall.'

'Stay there.'

I went to the stall.

'Excuse me, what kind of juice do you have?'

'Orange, peach, grapefruit.'

'Oh. And that's all?'

'That's all.'

'That's it.'

'No kelpie juice?'

'Well, kelpie's in all the drinks, young lady. The orange, peach and grapefruit just make it more flavoursome. So what'll it be?'

'It's OK. I'm not thirsty now.'

I went back to where I had left Martin. He'd gone. I looked and there he was, sprawled back on the grass with his new-found friends.

'Martin –'

'Hi, sis. You're back. Have you met my buddy Leo here?'

'Martin, we need to go.'

'Nah we don't. We don't need to go anywhere.'

'Martin!'

'Hey, buddy, your sister's giving me earache. I'm taking the guitar over there. You come and join us when she's gone.'

Martin's buddies stood up and left, leaving him and Leo, and Leo was gathering up his stuff too.

'Ah, see what you've done,' Martin said. 'And we were just getting to chill –'

'Martin –'

'What?'

'There was kelpie juice in that drink.'

'Was there? No kidding? That so? Then you should try it, sis. It's real good.'

'Is it?'

'Fantabulastic. Isn't it, Leo?'

'Sure thing, dude. Only wish I had some.'

'Me too,' Martin said. 'But my money's gone.'

'Don't worry, man,' Leo said. 'We can go off sky-swimming later and get some fresh kelpie all for ourselves.'

'Hey, awesome, dude!' Martin said. 'Awesome.'

Then I had an idea.

'Unless you two want to come to the boat,' I said.

Martin's eyes narrowed.

'The boat?'

'Peggy's cooking supper.'

'Well, I am getting hungry. You getting hungry, Leo?'

'Kelpie hungry, dude.'

'Well, that's what she's cooking. Kelpie fish and rice,' I said.

'Kelpie fish and kelpie rice! You hear that, Leo?'

'Awesome, dude,' he said.

'We going to go and get some of this kelpie rice and fish, dude?'

'And there's kelpie juice to wash it down too,' I said. And then – though I was worried I was maybe going too far – I added, 'And there's kelpie blancmange for pudding.'

'Wow! Kelpie blancmange, dude!' Leo said. 'I never even heard of that!'

'Then let's go and try it, dude,' Martin said, getting a little unsteadily to his feet and putting his shirt back on.

'Sure thing, buddy. Can't wait for this kelpie blancmange scene. You just hit me with that one.'

'Awesome, dude,' Martin said.

'Double awesome.'

And so they said goodbye to their friends in the park – I told them not to invite their buddies as there wouldn't be enough to go round – and off we went.

And, yes, as we walked along, everyone was so, so friendly. And solicitous too.

'Hey, you leaving us already, young people?'

'Just going to get some kelpie and fish and rice, thank you,' I assured them.

'No one's coercing you to leave now, are they? Because we don't like that here. We like everything nice and friendly and no hassles.'

'Oh no, we're not leaving. We're just having a little taste of kelpie and then we're coming right back,' Martin said. (And little did he know; and just as well.)

'Good to hear it, youngsters. We'll be looking out for you. And enjoy your kelpie.'

'Awesome.'

Everything was awesome, as far as I could make out. Even awesome was awesome.

'Hey, man,' Leo said, as we walked down to the harbour. 'What brought you dudes – like you and your sister, dude – to the island?'

'Oh, we were going to City Island to school – but we're not bothering with that any more. We're staying here and having ourselves some kelpie from now on? Aren't we, sis, dude?'

'You've got it, Martin, dude,' I said. 'We're staying here for the kelpie.'

'Awesome,' Leo said. 'Same story here. Small world, huh?'

'Awesomely small,' I said.

'Right on,' Leo said.

And then we were at the pontoon to our boat.

Peggy saw us coming. She took in Martin's and Leo's condition at a glance, and she saw me wink at her, and I knew she'd cottoned on.

'Hi, Gemma. Everything OK?'

'Fine, thanks, Peggy. I've just brought Martin and his new friend Leo back to the boat for some of that kelpie fish stew and rice you're cooking.'

'Oh, it's in the big pan right now,' Peggy said. 'Simmering down in the galley there.'

'And how's the old kelpie blancmange coming along, Peggy, dude?' Martin said.

'Just setting nicely,' she said. 'Why don't you take Leo below and have a look?'

'Hey, that would be awesome, dude. Let's go and inspect the makings. What do you say?'

'Lead me to the kelpie, man,' Leo said. 'Let's sharpen up the chopsticks and get stuck in.'

'You go down then, the both of you, and I'll be right down after,' Peggy said.

At which point Angelica nearly blew it. She was standing watching, wondering what was going on. Alain had twigged, but Angelica was a little more innocent.

'I didn't know we were having kelpie,' she said. 'I thought you warned us not to go anywhere near –'

'I was just kidding, my dear,' Peggy said. 'Everyone knows that kelpie's just the tops. Right, Martin?'

'It's awesome, Peg,' he said. 'No worries with the kelpie. You get a little kelpie down you and life's just, well . . . what is it, Leo?'

'It's awesome, man.'

'That's the word. Awesome. Let's go down below ships, man, and get our kelpie levels topped up.'

He led the way down below to the galley and Leo followed him.

The instant they were down, we slammed the hatch shut, and Peggy battened it down tight.

I won't record the language they used when they realised they'd been had and that there was no kelpie and that the ship was sailing and leaving the Friendly Islands way behind.

No, I won't tell you the expressions they used, but I can tell you this, the word awesome was not among them, though hell and damnation did figure in there occasionally.

We took off and sailed to meet the sleek boat waiting for us out in the sky. There was still a lot of thumping and banging and shouting coming from below, but it subsided and then there was the sound of snoring.

We tied up alongside and invited Leo's parents on board.

'He's all right, is he?'

'Looks it,' Peggy said. 'Just don't expect gratitude and you won't be disappointed. You want to open the hatch, Gemma?'

'Is it safe?'

'I can't see either of them trying to sky-swim it back to the Friendlies from here.'

So we unlocked and opened up the hatch and swung it back.

'Martin . . . Martin!' I yelled.

'Leo,' Peggy said. 'It's your mother.'

The snoring was replaced by grumbling and mutinous-sounding muttering, and then steps slowly clambered up the ladder, and first one, and then a second, set of bloodshot eyes appeared.

'Oh, my head –' Martin said. 'Something must have hit it.'

'I was tempted,' I said.

'Gemma –' Peggy said, disapprovingly. So I let it drop.

Leo looked even worse than Martin. His eyes were red with a tinge of yellow to them.

They came up and sat on deck. Peggy gave them water.

'Enjoy the Friendly Isles then, Martin?' she asked brightly.

'I *was* enjoying them,' he said. 'For a while.'

'Yes, the kelp's great until you stop eating it.'

'I think I'm going to be sick,' Leo said.

'Well, do be careful, dear,' his mother told him. But it was more a matter of urgency than caution.

'How come all the people on the islands aren't sick, Peggy?' I asked.

'They never stop eating the kelp. They start young and keep on going. You don't get withdrawal if you never stop.'

'And that's why they're so happy and friendly all the time?'

'Probably helps.'

'Hmm . . .'

Peggy looked at me dubiously.

'But we'd rather live in the real world, wouldn't we, Gemma?'

'I guess so,' I said.

'That's right.'

But I wasn't entirely sure about that, to be honest.

Leo's parents helped him over to their boat. He fell into a hammock and went straight back to sleep.

'We'll see you at City Island, Mrs Piercey,' his father called.

'No doubt you will. And we'll see you too. But you'll be there a good while before us in that boat, I think.'

'Well, thanks again for your help. We're more than grateful.'

'Our pleasure.'

We untied, waved them goodbye, and the sleek, stream-lined boat slipped away and was soon a kilometre or more ahead of us, moving as fast as a shark through the thermals of the sky.

'Well, let's hope he didn't get too strong a taste for it,' Peggy said.

'Who?'

'That Leo boy. It's OK if you catch it early, but any longer and you'll be back. The Friendly Isles will be a place you'll never get away from then.'

I looked at Martin with some concern. But he just grimaced.

'No,' he said. 'I don't think so. If I'd known that not having a care in the world made you feel like this, I'd never have thought it was such a good idea. Is there any more water there?'

'Sure,' I said. 'Or how about a kelpie juice?'

He headed for the rail in a hurry.

I didn't like to watch what happened. But I could certainly hear it.

It wasn't nice.

# 22

# a morning after

**MARTIN'S TURN TO SPEAK AGAIN:**

Yes. Travelling hopefully. That's what Peggy used to say. And she no doubt got it from somebody else who used to say it. We're all travelling hopefully, and often that part is better than the actual arriving.

We were on the last leg of the journey now, and soon we'd be there, and all the hopes would turn into realities, and maybe also into disappointments. I didn't see how City Island could ever live up to Peggy's promises for it. I thought I might just prefer to go on travelling and being hopeful forever. Always journeying but never arriving anywhere.

'How about that, Peggy?' I asked her, when I'd recovered from the worst of the effects of drinking kelpie juice. 'How about we just keep on going when we see City Island, go sailing on forever?'

'I think that might get a little tedious after a while, Martin.'

'I don't know.'

'The thing about travelling hopefully is that to do it, you need a destination. If you don't have anywhere to get to, or any expectations of the place, you're not travelling hopefully any more – just travelling . . . pointlessly.'

'I wouldn't mind.'

'Even Cloud Hunters, who never stop travelling, always have an object in view – the next cloud bank, the next island.'

'We could travel in the hope of . . . adventures.'

'You've not had enough of them yet, Marty?'

'I'll never have enough of them, Peg.'

'Well, I have. I'm going to lie down. You keep watch. Gemma can take the wheel.'

She went below. She was doing a lot of sleeping these days. Old age, she said, catching up with her, overtaking her even. But then she'd been old since I'd first known her; I didn't know why it was bothering her now.


I got a line and threw it over the side and Angelica came and joined me and we fished for lunch as the boat sailed along.

'Will we soon be there, Martin?'

'A few more days.'

'It's going to be strange.'

'Yes, I think so too.'

'Like nothing I've never known. Martin . . .'

'Hmm?'

'I've got to confess something to you – some of those rat-skinning stories I told you –'

'What about them?'

'I may have exaggerated a little. They weren't all, well – true.'

That made me smile.

'Yeah, I know,' I said.

'You knew?'

'Yeah. I know everyone thinks I'm gullible. But even I'm not that bad.'

'I only told them to you because you wanted me to.'

'I know. And they were pretty good stories as well. I really liked listening to them.'

'You did?'

'Yes. A lot.'

'You want me to tell you another one?'

'OK. If you've got any.'

'OK. One last and final rat-skinning story, before we get to City Island. Now, this is a true one, that really happened.'

'Absolutely,' I said.

But I never did hear it. We were interrupted. Alain had uncoiled himself from the hammock he had been swinging in and he loped over to the deck rail. He hopped up onto it, holding onto the rigging for balance. Then he pointed towards an approaching craft.

'Gemma – close the solars. It's Cloud Hunters again.'

She did as he asked. Out of the mist haze a cloud-hunting boat approached us, its decks wet with water and vapour, rolling heavily on the thermals, as if its holding tanks were full.

'Hey! Hey!'

Alain shouted and waved as he perched up on the deck rail. Figures appeared at the rail of the cloud-hunting boat – a man, a girl, a woman holding a child, and a lean and tattooed tracker.

'My God . . . I don't believe . . .'

And the next thing, he leapt from the rail and out into space – he air-swam a few dozen strokes and then he was by the cloud-hunting boat, and they were hauling him on board like a netted fish – like some long-hunted, rare and invaluable species that they had all but abandoned hope of ever finding.

Because it was his family. It was their boat.


Peggy must have felt the boat come to a stop, or heard the commotion, because she came back up on deck, stiff-kneed and little cranky.

'What have we stopped for? What's going on?'

Then she saw the Cloud Hunters, and she saw Alain among them.

'Well . . . well, now . . .'

But her smile soon changed, because the next moment the tracker in the Cloud Hunting boat was leaping from their boat to ours, a knife in his hand.

'I'll slit their throats,' he yelled. 'Every one of them!'

But Alain came after him.

'No!' he said. 'No! They aren't the ones who kidnapped me. They're the ones who saved me!'

And the tracker stopped in – well, his tracks – and

lowered the knife, which had been about to slit Peggy's throat, and he displayed a row of perfectly white teeth, framed in a smile, and said, 'Madam, how charming to meet you. What an absolute treat. You saved our boy from war and violence, all of which we loathe –'

'Evidently . . .' Peggy said.

'Allow us to express our undying gratitude.'

'I'm glad I'm still alive to receive your undying gratitude,' Peggy said. 'It was a close thing for a moment there.'

'Charmed, madam,' the tracker said. 'Totally charmed.'

And he reached out, took Peggy's hand, formally kissed it, then returned it to her, and all as if he was in a lounge suit and tie in some elegant drawing room, instead of half-naked, covered in tattoos and scars, and on a battered old boat in the middle of the sky.

Well, if we thought we were getting on our way any time soon after that, we thought wrong. Oh yes. We had to go on board the cloud-hunting boat and drink green tea and eat sky-shrimp, and then the best, sweetest water, kept for special occasions, was brought out. When that happened, Peggy – not wanting to be outdone with the hospitality – sent me back to our boat for our final bottle of old Ben Harley's private stash, and she presented it to the Cloud Hunters, who were all for opening it straight away, but she said no, not while small children were around, but maybe when their boat was safely tied up at a quiet island somewhere they should pop the cork and give it a go, and there'd be no cause to worry about any midges.

Alain sat cross-legged on the deck, just as the rest of his family did, and he recounted all that had happened to him, his abduction, his time in the Liberation Enlightenment Army as a child soldier, about the massacre (omitting the details as he didn't wish to upset his sister) and how he had finally found us and we had found him, and how we had spotted the cloud-hunting boat a while back, but thought that we had lost it.

'And where were you headed, Alain?' his mother asked. 'Where were you going to?'

'We're all going to City Island, ma'am,' I said. 'To school there. The government's paying for everyone to get educated who wants to be. It's all free and we're enrolling. Peggy's taking us there. She says it'll change our lives, and give us big chances. Right, Peggy?'

'It's more than that, Martin,' she said. 'You'll be able to understand and appreciate things.'

The Cloud Hunters fell silent. I think it was that word – education. Education widened your horizons, but it also took you away from your roots, your background; it could turn the past and your origins into places to which you would never again quite belong.

'Education, Eldar . . .' Alain's mother whispered to his solemn-faced father. 'Remember what we said –?'

'I know what was said,' he snapped.

Alain looked across at him.

241

'Of course, I shall stay here now,' Alain said. 'Help with the boat, hunt the clouds . . .'

His mother slowly shook her head. She turned to her daughter.

'Beth, get your things.'

'Why?'

'Just do as I tell you.'

She was the youngest of us all – apart from the baby. She couldn't have been more than nine.

'Dear lady,' Alain's mother said. 'Can you take our daughter with you too?'

Peggy looked horrified.

'Another one? I thought I was just getting rid of one, not acquiring another!'

'Mother, I'm staying here now. I'm not going with them.'

'You must, Alain. It's what we want for you.'

'It's not what I want.'

'Yes, it is – isn't it?'

And the sad truth was that she was right. He'd seen too much and known too much to go back to being a Cloud Hunter; he had things to do, a world to change, and he needed to discover how to do it. He could go into government, become a politician, fight for the rights of the unrepresented minorities – the Cloud Hunters, the sky-roaming gypsies, the rootless and homeless, the dispossessed. You can't unlearn what you know, and he'd learned too much already to go back.

'But we'll stay together . . . ?' he said.

'End of the term,' his father told him. 'City Island. You come to the western harbour and we'll be waiting for you.'

'And we'll go cloud-hunting . . . ?'

'Of course. What else would we do?'

'All right. Mother, Father, Corbis . . .' (Which, apparently was the name of the tracker.)

They embraced each other and said goodbye. Alain took his sister's hand and we returned to Peggy's boat.

'Alain –'

'Father?'

'The scars –' He indicated those unavoidable, unmistake-able scars that all Cloud Hunters bore, running from eyes to mouth. 'Wear them with pride.'

'I will,' Alain said. 'Always.'

And then the Cloud Hunters were gone, on their way.

Angelica was holding the little girl's hand.

'You don't have any scars, Beth, do you?'

'I'm too young yet,' she said. 'But I'll have them one day.'

Yet I doubted that. I didn't think she would. She'd be educated and absorbed into ordinary society – the first person of cloud-hunting origin not to go through the rites of initiation. No one would ever know where she had come from or who her parents had been.

She cried when the boat vanished into the distance. She seemed quite inconsolable. Alain tried to comfort her, but nothing worked.

'Beth,' Angelica said, 'would you like to hear a story?'

'What's it about?'

'Rat-skinning,' Angelica said.

'Is it a true story?' Beth said.

'Yes,' Angelica said. 'At least it is in places.'

In my opinion, that's about the best you can expect from any story – if it's true in enough places, then even if the rest is lies, it somehow becomes true all over.

'Come and sit on my lap and I'll tell it to you.'

'OK, Angelica,' I said.

'Martin! Not you.'

'Only joking . . .'

Beth sat by her and Angelica told her the story. The next time I looked into the sky, the Cloud Hunters could not be seen. They had evaporated, completely.

Peggy stood looking at us all.

'It's getting a little crowded on this boat,' she said. 'Still, never mind, we'll be there soon. You start up the solars then. I'm taking another nap.'

And she went back down below.

# 23

# city island, at last

**MARTIN STILL SPEAKING. BUT HIS LAST CHANCE:**

City Island was hard to miss, even long before you set eyes on it. You just followed the traffic. First there was us, sailing alone, and then we found we had company; a couple of craft appeared, heading in the same direction. And then, after a few more hours, there was real traffic, and the sky was filling with boats of all sizes and kinds – gunboats, garbage barges, cruise liners, factory boats, whalers and deep-sky trawlers, towing nets of writhing sky-fish. There was everything. I even saw a tiny rowing boat, which I'd never seen before. No solars, just one person and two big-bladed oars, with which you paddled your way across the sky.

Small satellite islands appeared. On one tiny isle sat a storage container, the kind you see on cargo ships. Somebody had given it windows and painted it green.

Writing on its side read: MADAME ACUSHLA: FORTUNES TOLD AND FUTURES READ.

'Peggy,' I called, seeing her emerge from the hatch after her nap, 'shall we get our fortunes told?'

'At ten Units a pop? I'll tell you your fortune for free.'

'What is it then?'

'If you don't start cooking soon, we'll all go hungry.'

'That's not proper fortune-telling, Peggy.'

'It's as good as anything they'll sell you.'

'OK, I'll start cooking in a minute.'

'What do you know? The boy can take a hint now. Well, that's progress.'

I went and put a stew on and left it on a slow boil, then came back up on deck.

It was amazing. There were little islands all around us now, and on each one people had set up stalls and shops, or they were hopping from boat to boat on tiny craft, peddling whatever they had to sell.

'Peggy – what is it? What's going on here?'

She was leaning on the rail, watching the free show, as were the others too.

'Market,' she said. 'Must be market day.'

'They all traders?'

'Of one kind or another.'

'Oh, look!'

Perched on a rock was a statue – a silver statue. But then, as I watched it, it came alive with abrupt, mechanical movements, changed its position, and froze again.

'Angelica, did you see that?'

'It's just a sky-performer,' Peggy said, unimpressed.

'Can we give the statue some money?'

'You got any?'

I flicked a couple of cents towards the statute. Its mechanical, robotic hands moved in flashes, snatched the coins from the air, made a gesture of thanks then froze again, and we sailed on.

A rowing boat drew up alongside us and without even asking, hitched on a tow line.

'Oh great,' Peggy said. 'A busker now. Hey, you. Get that grappling iron off my deck.'

But the man in the boat ignored her. He picked up a small guitar and cleared his throat.

'A little song, ladies and gentlemen, of my own composition. One to bring the tears to your eyes.'

And he started to sing. But he was so out of tune and off-key that he didn't just bring the tears to your eyes, he brought quite a lot of pain to your eardrums too.

'That's it,' Peggy said. 'You're going.'

And she unhitched the grappling iron.

'How about a sign of your appreciation, folks?' the busker shouted. 'Something in my cap?'

'Try sticking your head in it. Goodbye!'

And off he drifted to annoy somebody else.

'Useless,' Peggy said. 'He can't play and he can't sing. Why is it people are always attracted to professions they're no good at? And the things they are good at, they don't want to do.'

'Yes. Why is that, Peggy?' Gemma asked.

'The perverseness of human nature, I guess,' she said.

The busker, meanwhile, had latched onto another boat, and I heard his voice fade behind us, sounding as if he were strangling cats.

The market went on for two kilometres or more, full of colours and produce and sky-flowers and everything you could ever need. There was a boat with caged singing sky-fish, which warbled and whistled, and fluttered their fins.

'Cruel,' Angelica said. But there were people buying them, cruel or not.

It was quite a spectacle, and you didn't need to spend a cent to enjoy it; it was enough just to see it and to be there.

'Dust babies. Dust babies. Come and buy a dust baby. Never needs feeding. Never grows up and leaves you. Never breaks your heart. Never needs feeding or changing. Never cries or wakes you up. Sleeps through every night. Buy a dust baby.'

'Peggy, what's a dust baby?' I asked.

'I have no idea. A baby made out of dust, I suppose.'

'Who'd buy a dust baby?'

'Nobody I know.'

But the woman went on crying her wares, and there her dust babies were, set out for sale, with painted smiles on their faces, and wrapped in bright cloth. And a boat stopped, and somebody bought one. Then off they went, with their dust baby, looking pleased with their purchase, though I didn't know why.

Then we came to a corridor of sky-boats bearing red and white painted poles. *Haircuts*, their signs read. *Teeth pulled. Ears cleaned. Nails trimmed. Corns removed. Blisters burst.*

And down from them was a big sky-ship flying a red cross flag. *Private Hospital. Free Initial Consultation. Cosmetic Surgery. Remodelling. Cloud-hunting Scars Removed.*

'Never seen that before,' Peggy said. 'Thought it couldn't be done.'

'It can't,' Alain said, his fingers touching the scars on his face. 'They might fade a little, but they never go. And even if they did go from your skin, they'd still be there inside you.'

And then we were by the food stalls, and the smell made your mouth water.

'Shall we stop and get something, Peg?' I asked.

'I thought you were cooking,' she said.

I was, but my stew didn't smell as good as this. Still, it would have been a shame to waste it.

*Eat at Joe's. Drink at Pete's. Chow Down at Ibrahim's. Finest Delicacies at the Souproom Mush – Gourmet Roadside Dining.* There was food for every taste and palate, from around the whole sky-world.

We bought a few snacks to eat with the stew that was simmering down in the galley, then drifted on.

We passed a boat full of actors, who were putting on a play, staging it on the upper deck, while their audience watched from boats floating in the sky around them.

249

Next we came to Speakers' Rocks, where people commandeered a sky-rock each and tried to drum up an audience while they ranted and raved and expressed their views on the state of the world and what should be done about it.

On we went. The market stalls were fewer and further between now. We came alongside boat-building yards, where luxury sky-yachts were being constructed for wealthy owners. Then we heard the thumping of electric music, and we passed Night Club Island, which was shrouded inside an artificial globe that kept it in permanent darkness. Some people were leaving, making their way to sky-cabs, blinking in the light, while others were just arriving, all dressed in fine clothes, many looking weird and wonderful, and they nodded to the doorman, passed the approval test, and went inside to join the party that never came to an end.

'I've never seen anything like this, Peggy. This is unbelievable. Is this what we've been missing?'

'Martin,' Peggy said, 'believe me, you haven't been missing anything. Those people in there right now –' and she pointed to Night Club Island – 'are haunted by the feeling that somebody, somewhere else, is having a better time, and something's happening that they're missing out on. And that's how it goes. Once you start thinking you'll be happier somewhere else, you'll always think it, no matter where you are.'

And she went down below to rest.

But I didn't agree with what she'd said. Life had to be

better elsewhere sometimes. Or why were we going to City Island? That had been her idea, not ours. I hadn't even wanted to go there to start with. Though I did now. In fact, I was getting quite excited.

And then finally, there it was. We could see it, actually see it, in the distance, its towers and skyscrapers, its minarets and mosques, its churches and cathedrals, its temples and memorial tombs, its harbours and coastlines, its jetties and sky-marinas. Moored there were thousands of sky-boats, with more coming in, and many leaving. The sky was dense with traffic, and shimmering light danced in the sky, reflected off structures of glass and of shining, polished stone. City Island just gleamed like a jewel in space, some great, multi-faceted diamond. And as we approached, its colours changed in the light, iridescent and luminous, as if the island was inside a kaleidoscope, being turned by an unseen hand.

I'd never even imagined anything like it. It was like sailing through a long, empty sky, and suddenly stumbling across paradise.

We had arrived at the promised land.

# 24

# gemma takes the wheel

**GEMMA TELLS THE REST OF THE STORY:**

And there it was. We gathered at the prow, staring at the sights, with Martin almost falling over the rail from curiosity. But how were we ever going to land? I'd never seen so many boats. There were floating signs in the sky. KEEP RIGHT. KEEP LEFT. NO ENTRY. THIS WAY FOR DOWNTOWN. THIS WAY FOR C.I. HARBOUR. COMMERCIALS ONLY.

'Peggy –'

She'd come back up on deck.

'All right, I'll take it.'

She took the wheel. I was fine with sailing in the open sky, but not with this congestion.

'Where are we going to land?'

'We'll find somewhere.'

We followed other boats like our own, the small, private ones.

CITY ISLAND DOWNTOWN SKY-BOAT PARK: 20 UNITS A DAY.

'How much?' I said, when I saw that sign approaching. 'We'll only be able to stop for about five minutes.'

'That's for rich people who can't even be bothered with a short walk. We'll go to the public moorings. They used to be free.'

'How long since you were last here, Peggy?' Martin asked her.

'About ten of your lifetimes,' she said.

'Oh, let me work that out . . .'

'Just call it a long time and save yourself the trouble.'

'Has it changed?'

'Near unrecognisable,' she said. Then, 'Ah – there.'

Two signs mounted on a headland directed us to either MOORING: SHORT-TERM or MOORING: LONG-TERM.

'Which are we, Peggy? How long's long and how short's short?'

'Now there's a question to keep the philosophers busy. I don't really know. I'm only tying up long enough to drop you all off and see you settled, then maybe get some supplies, then back home.'

'Aren't you going to stay a while?' Martin asked.

'Yes, stay longer,' Alain said.

'Yes, please,' Beth, his sister, said.

'Stay forever,' Angelica told her.

'Why don't you, Peggy?' I said. 'Why not?'

She gave one of her sad old smiles.

'Well, maybe I will a few days, but I've got an island to take care of, and greenhouses that need tending, and who's going to put old Ben Harley in his place and save him from his follies and his private stash, if I'm not there to do it?'

'But who's going to look after us, Peggy?' Martin said, and he sounded four years old again, just like years ago.

'Marty, I don't know if you've noticed, but you and Gemma – as we've been sailing along now – you've learned pretty much to look after yourselves.'

'Have we?' Martin said, sounding surprised. Then he went quiet and got thoughtful. Because Peggy was right. We could look after ourselves. But it was thanks to her that we could do it.

'Peggy,' Alain said. 'Look there.'

There were more signs. SHORT-TERM MOORINGS: UP TO 3 DAYS. LONG-TERM MOORINGS: OVER 3 DAYS.

'Short-term should do it,' Peggy said. 'Three days is fine.'

So we turned to port and followed some other small craft towards the short-term mooring park.

As we did, I looked behind us. Just turning to starboard was a large sky-ferry, a brand-new, real comfortable-looking one. And I saw that the decks were lined with children, many of them our ages. There had to be a couple of hundred of them at the very least. They saw us and started shouting and waving, so we waved back. Then they headed off for the long-term moorings. As the boat levelled off, I saw its name on its side. It was called **ARTEMIS**. And along its hull, in bold letters, under its name, there was painted: CITY ISLAND SCHOOL. FREE BUS. SERVING ALL THE OUTLYING ISLANDS AND SETTLEMENTS.

And I just went cold.

'Peggy . . .'

'Uh huh?'

She was making out like she hadn't seen it.

'Peggy – did you see that?'

'What's that, darlin'?'

'Peggy – there's a bus. There's a school bus. Serving all the outlying settlements . . .'

'Really? That so?'

'Peggy, you can see it. Look. There it is. Just turning. Right there. It's huge. It doesn't even look full. There's a bus, Peggy. We could have come on the bus!'

'Oh . . . well now . . . yes . . . I guess you could.'

'Martin and I could have just got here on the school bus!'

'Ummm . . .'

'What's that?' Martin said, overhearing me. 'What are you saying? Hey, did you just see that big school bus?'

'We saw it, thank you. Peggy –' I said.

'What is it, Gem?'

'You knew –'

'What's that, darlin'?'

'About the bus. You knew, didn't you?'

'Well, I forget things. It's my age. What with the arthritis and the cramps, and I've been getting a touch breathless too recently . . .'

'Peggy, why didn't you just put us on the bus?'

She sighed.

'Gemma –'

'Well?'

'So many reasons, darlin'. I wanted to take you myself. And I wanted to see City Island one last time –'

'Why should it be the last time?'

'Shh, darlin'. Don't be angry now.'

'I'm not angry, Peggy, I just don't understand – I mean – this journey – everything we encountered – we could have sunk – been killed – you could have been killed – the minefields, the troll, that motel with those maniacs . . . We could have avoided all that. So, why?'

'Well – the school bus – what would you have learned on that?'

'Learned?'

'You'd just have been a passenger, darlin'. But on this boat, you've been crew, and captain too, sometimes. All of you. And the boy there –' she nodded towards Alain – 'and the two little ladies – where'd they be? One would still be a lonely soldier, and one'd be rat-skinning, and the other would be cloud-hunting and getting ready for her scars.'

'They could have got the bus too.'

'But they never would. It was meeting us that brought them here. Serendipity.'

'What's that?'

'Look it up in one of the big dictionaries they'll have in that school library there. Sometimes it's best to make your own way, darlin'. You can't beat your own steam for getting there. In my old opinion.'

I watched the big school ferry sail off towards its moorings, with all those children up on deck. I'd bet they'd all had comfortable berths on board, and catering, and showers, and organised activities, and all kinds of pastimes and amusements to keep them occupied on the long trip to City Island, as the ferry stopped off picking up its passengers for the term ahead from all the tiny and remote one-boat islands like our own.

But then they'd not seen what we had, or done what we had. And it was true what Peggy said. It had been an education.

'You don't mind, do you, darlin'?'

'No. I don't mind. I'm glad we made our own way.'

'It was fun, wasn't it?'

'Well . . . some of the time, Peg.'

'Well, that's only right. If it was fun all the time, it wouldn't be fun at all.'

'What?'

'Just think about it. We're here.'

A frantic parking attendant on a sky-bike was dashing around between the boats giving directions and pointing out moorings. We followed his instructions and tied up at a floating pontoon.

'Remember the number on the post or we'll never find the damned boat ever again.'

'G27.'

'I'm going to write it on the back of my hand,' Peggy said, squinting. 'Anyone seen my glasses?'

'Peggy,' I pointed out, 'you don't wear glasses.'

'Then maybe,' she said, 'it's time I did.'

Well, I don't know about the others, but I certainly felt like some country cousin from the out-sticks as we made our way through the streets of City Island and headed for the enrolment at the school.

There were people so fine and elegant and dressed in such fashions and styles as I'd never even imagined, let alone seen. And they had such ways about them too, ways of walking and talking, and gesturing and standing. You felt a little crushed just seeing them, like you were a simpler, less complicated being, and would never attain their dizzying heights of sophistication.

Peggy must have read my mind, because she said, 'Gemma, don't go getting taken in by the posers now.'

'What's a poser, Peggy?'

She nodded at the people in the wild, extravagant clothes.

'They are. Scratch 'em and they're no different to you and me. All veneer and no substance. Flesh and blood, that's all. I think we're down this way now.'

It wasn't hard to find the way, you just followed the other parents, the other guardians, the other children, the other families – which is what we were too – a family of a kind.

ENROLMENT

Peggy led us up to a desk. I looked around me. Some of the other people were arriving with big suitcases and luggage on wheels. All we had was a bag each. Alain had next to nothing.

258

'Don't you worry about that,' Peggy said, mind-reading again. 'All's provided. And I'll be leaving you some money.'

'Peggy, we haven't got any money.'

'Ben Harley's not the only one with a private stash. I've been saving it up for you – you and Marty. To tide you over.'

'Peggy –'

'No, I don't want it. It's for you. We're going to put it in a bank account later where it'll be safe and you can use it as you need.'

'Peggy –'

'Now don't go thanking me or I'll be getting embarrassed.'

We shuffled along in the queue, then we were next.

'Names, please.'

'Piercey,' Peggy said. 'Gemma and Martin Piercey.'

The woman at the desk checked her list.

'OK. They have places reserved.'

'And could you take three more?' Peggy said.

'Three!'

'If you can?'

'Ages?'

Alain, Beth and Angelica gave their ages.

'Are they Pierceys too?' the woman asked.

'In spirit,' Peggy said.

'OK – just let me check . . .'

'Government does say free schooling for any child as wants it . . .' Peggy said.

'Yes, it's just whether we have the places at this particular – oh yes. That should be all right. Yes. They're accepted.

Here are your name tags and your form numbers. You'll find monitors in the next room holding cards up. You find the one with the card number matching your age and just join them for now.'

'Then thank you kindly,' Peggy said.

'Thank you. Next!'

'This way, Peggy. In here.'

But she didn't follow.

'No, I'll be leaving you to it now, darlin' –'

Sudden shock filled me. I felt trembly, a bit sick. This couldn't be it, already, so abruptly, so absolute.

'Peggy, no –'

'There's no one holding up a sign in that room with my age on it, darlin'.'

'But, Peggy –'

'You can't just go, Peggy –'

'No, you can't –'

'You can't –'

'No –'

'I'm not just going. I'm going to be waiting here. You go and find your rooms and get settled and then you meet me back here and we'll all go out for dinner. How's that?'

So that was what we did.

We went out for dinner to a restaurant in City Island, and Peggy ordered wine, and she said we all had to try it, even at our age, though she did water it down a little. She made a toast.

'To getting educated,' she said.

'To Peggy,' I said.

So we drank to both.

It was strange leaving her. We all walked her back to the marina and made sure she got on board OK, as she'd drunk most of the wine, to be honest, and was a little unsteady on her old feet.

'Thank you, darlin's – that was wonderful. Couldn't have had a better send-off.'

'But you're not going yet, Peggy? You're not sailing now?' I said, panicking again.

'Oh, no. You come and see me tomorrow. We'll say a proper goodbye then. Oops! Who left that step there? Oh my.'

'And we'll be back for the long holidays, Peggy,' Martin said. 'You don't have to come and get us. We'll take the school bus. And we'll write –'

'Sky-post ain't exactly regular –' she said.

'We'll still write though –'

'That'll be lovely, darlin' – I'll look forward to that. Gemma, Martin, you say goodnight to your great-great-grand – whatever – you say goodnight to me now.'

And we did. We each gave her a hug and a kiss.

'Thanks, Peggy. For everything – for looking after us – bringing us up – giving us a home –'

'Oh no – I've got to thank you – the pleasure was all mine – I have to tell you – the day you arrived and those Cloud Hunters brought you – I was in more than two minds – but I wouldn't have done without you for the world – nor all the islands in it.'

'I love you, Peggy.'

'I love you too, of course I do, why wouldn't I? But don't keep saying it or you'll make me cry.'

'Love you, Peggy –'

'My Martin, my little boy – only not so little now – my Gemma – my little girl –'

It took us a while to all dry our eyes and get disentangled. Alain, Beth and Angelica were tactfully waiting out of the way. Then they all said goodbye to Peggy too. But not too seriously. After all, we were coming back to wave her off tomorrow. School didn't start properly for another two days, so we wouldn't be missing anything important.

'What time shall we come tomorrow, Peggy?'

'Oh, not too early. I shan't be sailing before noon at the earliest.'

'Will you be all right on your own?'

'Sure I will. I'm tough as old boots by now.'

'Indestructible, eh, Peggy!' I said.

'That's it, darlin'. Indestructible.'

But she wasn't. None of us is.

The others couldn't come the next day. As they hadn't enrolled into the school in advance they were stuck with extra form-filling, so it was just Martin and me who made our way to the marina to see Peggy off on her journey home.

Her boat was alone on the pontoon. The other boats which had been there previously had already sailed.

'Peggy!' I called, as we tramped up the walkway. 'We're here. Are you up?'

'Maybe she's gone to get a few supplies,' Martin said.

'Or she's sleeping off last night's dinner. Go and see if she's down below and give her a shake.'

'OK.'

Martin went down below and I tidied up a little on deck and checked the solar panels and made sure the water tanks were full.

'Gemma –'

'What is it?'

'Gemma –'

'Martin – what is it?'

'I can't wake her, Gemma. She won't wake up.'

## 25

# by invitation

**GEMMA: FINAL WORD:**

'My name is Gemma Piercey, and just as you are now, I was also once a pupil at this school. And just as you will too, I grew up, and went out into the world. And I've been asked by the headmistress to return as the annually invited speaker to give the keynote address – as you may also have the honour to do one day. So I shall do my best not to bore you. And that'll mean keeping it brief, which I will.

'I came here rather late to start a formal education. I was already in my teens. But the teaching was good and I soon caught up, as did my brother, Martin. We were orphans, who had lost our parents when we were very young, and we were brought up by a rather wonderful old lady called Peggy Piercey, who gave us her name and looked after us on a remote little island that she owned, at the edges of the Outlying Settlements.

'Peggy was related to us, but so remotely as to be almost too far away to see. She was a great-great-grand-aunt, or something along those lines. She had no real reason to take us in and look after us, but she did, for which I am eternally grateful.

'We could have remained on that island indefinitely, and I might be there still, if Peggy hadn't been such a great believer in getting an education. So she got us accepted as pupils at this school, and we set off one day to travel here – Peggy, myself, and my younger brother Martin – who now works as a sky-pilot for the Inter-Island Lines, and is captain of one of their largest cruisers.

'It wasn't an easy journey, and we picked up a few other potential pupils along the way – all now quite eminent and well known in their own fashion. One was Alain Qualar, our first Member of Parliament to have come from a cloud-hunting family; another his sister, Beth, who you might know as a singer. And, maybe most famous of all, Angelica Tanner, the writer, whose series of children's books about the life of a girl apprentice rat-skinner unexpectedly proved to be the publishing sensation of the year. I understand that there is already a film in the works and other books to follow. In fact I probably only got asked to speak today as Angelica was too busy – only joking.

'Anyway, I can't tell you that I'm rich, or that I'm famous. But I don't know if that is the point. For those of you who don't know about me, I'm an eye surgeon who works for the Free Hospital Ship. I spend most of my time travelling around the system, and along with my colleagues, we treat numerous people who, without our help, would lose their sight. We don't charge for our service and we're funded purely by public donation.

'I always wanted to do something to help other people, ever since I came to City Island, and I've sometimes wondered why that is. And I guess I know. An education is a wonderful thing. But a school can't teach you everything. Some things in life you learn without knowing you're learning them. They rub off on you – like brushing against a flower and the pollen sticking to you – and you carry them with you. You learn from the people around you, and if you're lucky, those people will be the ones who want the best for you.

'So this is the other reason I am here. Not just to talk to you about the future, but to express my gratitude to our great-great-grand-aunt, and to this school, for all they both gave us.

'So that's it. I'm keeping it short, as promised. I don't have any wonderful advice. Just make the most of it, that's all. This is your chance and many people never get one. But I did. And you've got one too.

'And lastly, there's an old boat down at the marina, in the floating museum there. You might want to go and visit it when you have some free time. It's called the *Voyager*. It's quite small and nondescript, but it's full of history, and there's something special about it. If you stand on the deck, you can almost feel its past. And you can read about the journey it made. Of course, no one would even contemplate such a journey on a boat that size now. They used to call those little boats sky-runners, and it was one of the last of them. And I guess that is my claim to fame. I sailed on it, on the last of the sky-runs. I wouldn't be here now, if it hadn't been for that little boat and for the lady who owned it.

'I guess that was maybe the most wonderful time of my life, when I look back on it. I learned so much and I saw so much. I didn't know how special it was. Nor how special the lady was who adopted us and looked after us. So that's all I have to say really. Just take your chance, and do your best. And don't be afraid to tell the people you love that you love them. And do it while you still can. Good luck. Just tell them while you can. Because you never know when they might be taken from you. It's not very original, I know. But it's still true and still pertinent. And always will be, I guess.

'Thanks for listening. I think we're due to get some lunch now – which is always something to look forward to.

'And, oh, before I forget. If you do visit the *Voyager*, down at the marina museum, you'll no doubt run into a sky-cat there, who lives on board. He's been there a long time and no one can coax him to leave. But he's well fed and looked after. Anyway, you be sure to make a fuss of him and pet him a little, and he'll be your friend. He answers to the name of Botcher.

'I think he's waiting for someone to come home.

'And can't understand that they never will.'